WITHDRAWN 4/89

WITHDRAWN

Children
of the River

Children
of the River

LINDA CREW

**Delacorte
Press**

Published by Delacorte Press
Bantam Doubleday Dell Publishing Group, Inc.
666 Fifth Avenue
New York, New York 10103

Copyright © 1989 by Linda Crew

All rights reserved. No part of this book may
be reproduced or transmitted in any form or by any means,
electronic or mechanical, including photocopying, recording
or by any information storage and retrieval system,
without the written permission of the Publisher,
except where permitted by law.

The trademark Delacorte Press® is registered
in the U.S. Patent and Trademark Office.

Library of Congress Cataloging in Publication Data

Crew, Linda.
Children of the river.

Summary: Having fled Cambodia four years earlier
to escape the Khmer Rouge army, seventeen-year-old
Sundara is torn between remaining faithful to her
own people and adjusting to life in her Oregon
high school as a "regular" American.
[1. Asian Americans—Fiction. 2. Khmers—Fiction]
I. Title.
PZ7.C86815Ch 1989   [Fic]   88-20401
ISBN 0-385-29690-8

Book design by Andrew Roberts

Manufactured in the United States of America
March 1989
10 9 8 7 6 5 4 3 2 1
BG

For SAM-OU KOH REANG
And for all those who see
not only with their eyes

ACKNOWLEDGMENTS

Children of the River is a work of fiction and the characters do not represent real individuals. It is, however, based on historical realities.

I would like to thank the following people for sharing their experiences and insights with me:

Dr. John Berry, Tom Cope, Siv Chhing Chang, Vuthy Koh, Prakap Kuy, Sovanna Kuy, Srey Mom Pich, Chanthu Sam, Khen Reang, Khansinaro Reang, Dominic Tagliavento, Simsundareth Tan, Dr. Earl Van Volkinburg, and Dr. Michael Wong.

LINDA CREW
January 28, 1988
Corvallis, Oregon

CHAPTER *1*

April 17, 1975

For a brief time, it seemed the New Year had brought good fortune to the household of Tep Naro in the Cambodian village of Réam: a fat-cheeked new daughter born to his wife, Soka.

The birth itself had not been an easy one, however, and Naro and Soka were glad their young niece Sundara had come down from Phnom Penh to help.

On the day after the birth Sundara sat rocking the new baby in the wooden swing on the front porch. The afternoon air was soft and warm; a pleasant breeze wafted up from the gulf. Nuzzling the baby, she breathed in the sweet newborn smell. Such a nice plump little body. Such a thick thatch of black hair.

]1[

In the hammock, Sundara's six-year-old cousin, Ravy, lay nibbling leftover sticky rice cakes and entertaining his little brother Pon with a boat he'd made of knotted straw.

A sad love song played on the radio and Sundara kept time, lazily dangling her rubber thong from her toe, thinking of Chamroeun, the boy she'd left back in the city two weeks ago.

"I want to go fight the Communists," he'd told her that last night in Phnom Penh, the night before her father had spirited her through the teeming, refugee-choked boulevards to the airport. Hearing these words as the shells from the Communist guns screamed at the city's edge had terrified her. But now it seemed only a bad dream. Here, safe in her relatives' fishing village, lulled by the rustling of the coconut palms, she could almost imagine this as simply another vacation. The war that had dominated their lives seemed so far away, so unreal . . .

When the baby fussed, Sundara jiggled her, clicking her tongue as she'd seen the other women do. This seemed to calm the little one. Sundara smiled. She was beginning to feel quite capable, much older than thirteen. "Don't worry," she whispered to the baby, whom she had already grown to love, "I'll take care of you."

Suddenly the radio music stopped for an announcement . . . something about a new government. Then a terse exchange, a brief commotion. Then, nothing. Sundara shifted the baby to one arm and turned the dial.

"That's odd," she murmured to Ravy. "It's gone dead."

A moment later two men hurried past the house. Then, a panicky family.

Sundara rose. "What's happening?" she called. "Where's everyone going?"

"Get out! Get away! The Communists! The Khmer Rouge! They've taken Phnom Penh and they're coming here!"

The Communists! Hot fear burned her chest. She whirled and ran into the main room.

"Grandmother! Younger Aunt! Wake up! The Khmer Rouge are coming! Everyone's running away!"

Soka moaned, more in pain than alarm. "What does Naro say?"

"Naro's not here! He's still at work."

Soka shifted on her wooden bed. "I can't go anyway. Not *now*."

Grandmother peered out the window. "Just wait for Naro, child. My son is the head of this family. I'm sure he'll tell us this is nothing."

Clutching the baby, Sundara paced the house. The servant girl had fled down the back steps, leaving supper to burn. How much time did the rest of them have?

The trickle of people in the street became a stream.

Watching them, Grandmother sniffed. "I, for one, don't plan to leave my home just because the government might change hands once again. What has that to do with an old woman like me?"

Brave words, Sundara thought, but Grandmother had not seen the billboards all over Phnom Penh, the hideous picture that warned what the Khmer Rouge would do if they came to power: A woman stabbed with a dagger, her sarong torn away, her legs—

"Don't just stand there, you foolish women!" Naro jumped off his roaring motorcycle, let it fall in the dusty yard. "Haven't you heard?" He hauled the two-wheeled cart from under the house. "Throw our things in this. Now!"

]3[

Sundara dashed into the house. Laying the baby on a mat, she tossed clothes into a satchel. "We're leaving, Younger Aunt."

"But I can't!" Soka protested. "It's impossible!"

Naro ran in. "Up, Soka! Hurry!" He flung open the teakwood chest, rummaged for a packet at the bottom.

"Are you crazy, Husband? Have you forgotten? I just had a baby! I'm still bleeding. If you make me go now, I will die!"

Sweat beaded his forehead. "If we stay, we will *all* die. Everyone who worked for the United States must get out *now!*" He turned on Sundara and Grandmother. "You two, grab that basket of dried fish, the small gas stove . . ." He scooped Soka from her bed and bore her down the steps.

The baby fussed frantically at the commotion. Sundara snatched up her checkered *krama* and lashed the red-faced bundle to her breast, then rushed through the house grabbing dishes, food, mats. Just one thing more. The parasol. Her chest clutched tight. *Phnom Penh! Oh, God, what about her family, what about Chamroeun— No. No time for that now . . .*

"You're killing me!" Soka was screaming down in the yard. "We haven't even had the childbirth ceremonies yet. We cannot leave without purifying the house!"

Grandmother tugged at Naro's sleeve. "She's right, my son. The spirits won't like it if—"

"Shut up! Both of you! Now hurry!"

Pon burst out crying.

Sundara threw everything into the cart and plopped the toddler on a sack of rice. She seized a cart handle and Grandmother, in a daze, did the same. Together they shoved the heavy contraption after Naro, who staggered ahead toward the wharf under Soka's sobbing weight. Behind them, Ravy struggled to keep up, bravely lugging the pot of supper they'd yanked from the fire as an after-thought.

"Where are we going?" he kept calling.

No one answered.

People crowded on the pier with their squalling children and hastily gathered possessions, stumbling in panic up the gangplank to a large freighter. A few men rolled motorcycles on board; one family pushed a refrigerator. All was shouting and confusion. Where were they going and for how long? Who should be let on? Who must be left behind? Somehow Naro knew the right people: his family would be allowed to board.

Night was coming on fast. The wind whipped Sundara's hair about her face as she gripped the baby in her *krama* with one arm, balanced Pon on her opposite hip and, swept by the mass of people, began the long, sloping climb up the gangplank to the ship.

For hours, it seemed, she had been picking her way among the people crammed together on the hot metal deck, trying to shield the baby from the blazing sun with her bleached-out parasol. Three weeks they'd been on the sea, and Soka was ill. Sundara had been left to care for the little one alone.

She scanned the crowd. Surely there was one nursing mother among these hundreds of people, a woman who could help her. Ah! Over there, sitting by the motor-cycle . . .

Sundara bowed awkwardly before the young mother and her child. "Excuse me, please. My aunt is very sick and her milk has dried up. Now her little one grows weak too." She pulled back the blue-checkered *krama*. "See how strange and dried out her skin is? Look. Even her soft spot sinks in."

The woman winced, then averted her eyes. She held her own baby a little closer.

Sundara licked the salt from her cracked lips. "I was wondering . . . could you . . . ?"

"I'm sorry," the woman whispered, "I would, but . . . Oh, this is all so terrible. I'm not getting enough to drink myself. Soon I'm afraid I won't have milk for my own."

Sundara nodded, swallowing hard. Everyone had the same story. Their own families had to come first. She covered the baby and moved on. Heaven protect her, the baby grew lighter by the moment, her life running out in diarrhea that stained Sundara's cotton sarong in reeking brown streaks. How limp she was, and so silent. . . .

Oh God, what to do?

She went down to the hold where they guarded the donated supplies and found it crowded with people pleading for extra shares. She pushed into the weary crush. Breathless with the heat, she finally squeezed through to one of the men in charge.

"Our baby is so sick. Can you give me something for her?"

"Everyone's sick," he replied impatiently, showing bad teeth. His breath stank. "Everyone wants something extra. There's not enough extra for all seven hundred!"

Sundara shut her eyes, faint with disappointment and lack of air.

"For the love of heaven," said a woman. "Can't you even give her an extra packet of milk?" Her voice softened. "Poor child. No grown-ups to help you?"

"They all have the seasickness," Sundara whispered.

The man's mouth twisted. "Well, here then." Grudgingly, he shoved a packet at her.

Tears squeezed from the corners of her eyes.

"*Now* what's the matter?" he demanded.

"Thank you. I'm grateful, but . . . I think that's partly what made her sick, because before I had to mix milk in water without boiling it first." She took a deep breath, gathering courage. "I need medicine."

"Medicine! Do you think this is a hospital? Do I look like a doctor? I wouldn't know what to give you if I had it." He glanced around. "That Thai ship donated these. Sugar water or something." He held up a glass bottle of clear liquid. "Although I don't know what they expect us to do with them since this is for putting in the veins and we don't have any needles."

"I'll take it," Sundara said quickly. It was liquid; it looked clean. She had to try something.

"All right. But one thing—we don't need any more diseases than we've got. If that baby dies, throw it overboard right away."

What! Throw the baby— Horrible man. She snatched the bottle and struggled out through the press of people, holding the little bundle tighter than ever. This baby *couldn't* die. She wouldn't let her. She would do anything. She would find a way to feed her. She would pray to God, promise to shave off all her long hair in gratitude if only the child would live. . . .

Nothing had changed back at their tiny section of the deck. Ravy huddled dejectedly with Pon, whose eyes were taking on the same sunken look as his baby sister's. The three grown-ups sprawled against the sack of rice, oblivious to the beating sun. Sundara squinted upward, hand shading her eyes. The tarp the ship people tried to rig had

LINDA CREW

been ripped away by the hot wind. No shade, and nothing she could do about it. Well, she could at least try to clean up their patch of deck. She pulled a sarong from their satchel and swabbed at the new vomit. Hurry. Mustn't let it bake on the hot metal. Oh, no! Now little Pon had diarrhea too.

"Help me, Ravy." She propped Pon against the suitcase and handed Ravy the baby. She unpeeled the bottle's silver seal and yanked out the stopper, dividing the liquid between a cup and the baby bottle she'd begged from another family. She handed Ravy the cup for Pon, quickly looking away, unable to bear those big, questioning six-year-old eyes.

"Now, you must drink," she coaxed, cradling the baby again. "Please, *please* drink." But the tiny head fell back from the bottle. "Oh, Little One, can't you swallow? No, no, don't let it dribble away . . ."

CHAPTER 2

September 7, 1979

The third-floor classroom window was open, allowing a wispy thistle seed to float in on a breath of late summer air. Sundara clenched her hands on her desk and watched the spinning puff drift by. When you saw one of these, you could make a wish. An American girl who worked beside her in the strawberry fields had told her that. Sundara closed her eyes. *How I wish I had not written that poem.*

Every muscle in her body was tense. She never dreamed Mrs. Cathcart would read these first English papers aloud.

"In conclusion," the teacher read from a student's paper, "let us choose our own lunch menus. A lot less food would end up in the garbage if we did."

]9[

"Yay," came one listless voice. This was the sixth paper on cafeteria food, and only one—the blond boy's—had been truly funny. The students were sinking ever lower in their hard wooden chairs, nothing much having caught their attention since one girl's daring essay on why kids were entitled to birth control counseling without their parents' permission. How Sundara's face had flamed at that! She could just hear her aunt Soka: "These American girls, going to bed with men before they're married. . . . Why, if they were mine, I'd throw them out so fast . . ."

"And now I'd like to share a very special piece of work by Sundara Sovann." Mrs. Cathcart smiled at Sundara. "If she doesn't object."

I do object! Sundara longed to cry. But of course she couldn't. Deny a teacher's request? Impossible. She glanced behind her. Thirty pairs of eyes bored into her, waiting. True, one girl had written about her cat dying, but the rest of these eyes belonged to a puzzling group of people who had chosen video games, school dress codes, and football team conduct rules as topics that concerned them most deeply. Sundara sighed. Even now, four years after leaving Cambodia, she could not seem to understand the Americans.

Lowering her eyes, focusing once more on her scratched, damp-palmed hands, she finally nodded.

"We are the lost, we are the lonely
So far from our beloved land
We are the children of the Mekong
Who will not see that mighty river again
O Kampuchea
The blood of our people
Has stained you

The bones of our people
Lie in unmarked graves
But the love of the ancient Khmers
Will live in our hearts
We will not forget you
Even from this new place
On the far side
Of the earth."

Silence. Endless silence. She did not look up as the teacher slipped the offending paper into her view. *Very good,* Mrs. Cathcart had written in red pencil, but the praise was small compensation for this embarrassment. Why hadn't she written about something safe, like the others?

She couldn't wait to get away when the bell rang, away from all those staring eyes. Threading through the crowds, she hurried down the two flights of stairs to the girls' locker room to dress for PE, her last class of the day.

"Sundara, what's wrong?" It was Kelly, her chemistry lab partner, peering at her. Kelly's glasses made her eyes look huge.

"Not'ing," Sundara said. She could never master the *t-h* sound.

"Come on. You're acting like somebody's after you."

Sundara forced herself to smile calmly as she gathered her long black hair into her fist and snapped a clip around it. "Not'ing is wrong." She and Kelly had been friendly since the seventh grade, when they'd met at the church that sponsored Sundara's family. Even so, Sundara had never spoken of her homesickness to Kelly. Not to anyone. When they'd first come to Oregon, she had been too busy learning to live in America, and the kind ones, like Kelly, had been too busy trying to teach her.

Perhaps because of her faltering English, no one had tried, at first, to coax out her story, no one except that boy with pimply red skin. "How many people did you see get killed?" he'd asked her, eyes glittering. She shuddered, glad he was at her old high school. She would have hated to have him hear her poem.

"So how's it going?" Kelly asked. "Finding your way around okay?"

Sundara nodded. She hadn't been happy when she learned that moving to a new house would mean enrolling at the other high school. She was just getting to know people at Kennedy. But it would be all right. Changing schools was nothing compared to changing countries.

Out on the field, she kicked the soccer ball with the others, but she couldn't concentrate. Now, because of her putting those words on paper, far too many people knew her thoughts. Which was worse, to walk around with everything held inside so that no one really knew you? Or to have these feelings exposed to the whole world? Her aunt and uncle would be most displeased if they knew of this. Hadn't they warned her against telling their troubles or sounding ungrateful for their new life here? Hadn't they insisted the first English words they learned must be "Thank you very much" and "Very happy to be here"?

Even after PE, she was still so distracted, she stood waiting for the bus by the curb a minute before remembering her aunt had sent her with the station wagon that morning so she could hurry home for tomato picking.

She turned into the subdivision where their small house sat in a row with the others, the young, twiglike trees not yet large enough to soften the raw newness of the neighborhood. *I hope Soka won't notice I'm late,* she thought. They had to keep to American time now. Three-thirty meant three-thirty exactly.

But when Soka flung open the door and ran out onto the driveway, she was clearly upset by something more important than Sundara's being five minutes late. "Niece!" she cried in Khmer. "Quickly! Come see this letter. Grandmother and I can do nothing but weep all day!" She hurried Sundara in, hardly giving her time to place her shoes on the mat by the door.

Sundara set her books on the kitchen counter and followed her aunt into the living room. Grandmother crouched on a straw mat, her close-cropped gray head bowed in despair, touching the paper in question as if trying to decipher the strange markings with her gnarled fingers alone.

Soka took the letter from her and thrust it at Sundara, who by now was trembling in sick anticipation, her mind whirling with the awful possibilities.

"Will you boys turn down that foolishness?" Soka called to her sons in the next room. "We cannot think." The hysterical cheering of a TV game show snapped off. Silence.

Swallowing hard, Sundara unfolded the paper. *The Office of the United Nations High Commissioner for Refugees, Thailand.* News of her parents, her brother and sister? No, scanning the brief lines, she saw only the name of another aunt, Soka's sister Valinn, who, at the end of the last dry season, had scrambled down Khao-I-Dang mountain into a Thai border camp and collapsed in a malarial stupor.

Sundara let out a tentative breath. "Younger Aunt, why are you so upset? It's not the news we want, but there is still hope, isn't there? It says here they need more information before we can sponsor her. They want us to—"

"But look. *Look.*" Soka jabbed a finger at the crackly onionskin paper. "I've taken this to Prom Kea to tell me what the English says. And you see? 'Do not contact us again about this case.' Who can we turn to if not the United Nations? Prom Kea is telling his friends about this too. Everyone is very upset."

"Younger Aunt—"

"Do they expect us to simply forget our families? My own sister? Oiee!"

"Younger Aunt, do you see this word? *Hesitate.* It says, 'Please do not hesitate to contact us again.' It means just the opposite of what you thought. It's all right to write them more letters. They *want* us to."

Soka's round face went blank, then lit with a broad, embarrassed smile. "Oh!" She put her palms to her cheeks. "Oh, I was so scared." She dropped to a squat next to Grandmother. "It's a mistake," she said into the old woman's ear. "The United Nations will still try to help us." She allowed herself a moment to enjoy the relief, then jumped up. "That Prom Kea! He thinks he knows English so well! But then, I am too glad about this to be angry. Quick, Niece, change your clothes. There's some cold corn for you in the kitchen." Then she called to the boys. "Ravy, Pon, come now! Grandmother, are you ready? We will pick many tomatoes tonight and send the money we earn to Valinn. Hurry, *hurry,* or the Lam family will pick the whole field before we get there."

Perfect weather for picking Mr. Bonner's fall raspberries and cherry tomatoes: warm, sunny, and dry. Sundara

Children of the River

crouched over her row, her quick fingers stripping the small orange tomatoes from the vines. It hadn't taken them long to harvest the small berry patch, and the tomatoes were now thunking into the plastic buckets with a steady intensity.

"Pon!" Sundara called, brushing away the mosquito that tentatively tickled her lower lip. "I need an empty one."

Her six-year-old cousin picked his way through the scratchy vines with another cardboard flat in which he'd placed a dozen Styrofoam pint boxes. Sundara spilled the bucket of tomatoes into the flat.

"Fore!" On the other side of the blackberry and poison oak thickets that lined the fence, golfers strolled about the adjacent course, playing their odd game. To Sundara, the women golfers always seemed so brown and wrinkled. Americans certainly had funny ideas about what looked nice. She had even seen one blond girl pruning berry vines for Mr. Bonner in a bathing suit! Her skin was burned a deep brown, but she only seemed concerned with her nose, which was smeared with some kind of thick white paste. Sundara stood and retied the strings of her broad-brimmed straw hat. She did not want the sun to darken her skin, and avoided even the late afternoon rays.

She stooped back to work, slapping another mosquito on her cheek. "Here's a full one," she called. Ten-year-old Ravy carried the loaded flat to Mr. Bonner's truck, where Grandmother sat dreaming and sorting out the occasional bad tomato.

Sundara's fingers flew. This was the last crop of the season and the best money-maker of all, an opportunity Soka did her best to guard. If all the refugees they knew who wanted work came to Mr. Bonner's small farm, no single family would earn much at all. Sundara had often heard Soka turn vague when the others tried to coax it out of her.

"Ah, the cherry tomatoes again," they would say with more than a trace of resentment. "And where can you possibly be picking raspberries in September? Are you trying to make your first million this year?"

Soka would help these others if she could, Sundara knew, but their own family had to come first. As long as Valinn was still in Khao-I-Dang they had to send money to her. And what of the others in Kampuchea itself, the ones from whom they'd had no word? If they were alive, they might be needing money to bribe an escape. So Soka kept news of work to herself. And since Mr. Bonner couldn't communicate well with most of the Asians, she exerted a fair amount of control over how many families came to pick.

Tonight, only the Lam family worked alongside them. The Lams had come to America just last year after escaping Vietnam by boat. They were Chinese, and as Soka always pointed out with a grudging admiration, the Chinese could practically smell money to be made. You could not expect to keep work secret from them. Lam Ming, the father, picked with admirable speed, even though Sundara thought it must hurt his pride to do this work at all, having managed his own wholesale produce company in his homeland.

Faster, *faster*, Sundara urged herself, working steadily to the clank of the plastic bucket handles, the drumming of tomatoes on the bucket bottoms, the distant chug of Mr. Bonner's tractor as he disked under an early corn patch.

At six Sundara's Uncle Naro appeared, having parked his new Ford near the Bonners' house rather than dirty it on the dusty farm road. He had changed from office to work clothes, and carried a sack of Big Macs for the children.

Soka glanced up just long enough to point out the next unpicked row to her husband. Naro kicked off his thongs, smoothly curled into a crouch, and proceeded to strip tomatoes into his bucket like a well-oiled machine.

Sundara sat down next to Grandmother. She would have to eat quickly. It didn't seem right, taking too much time when Soka refused to stop even for a minute. But how Sundara's body longed for rest! She could have laid herself in the dirt and been asleep instantly.

"Are you hungry, Grandmother?"

The old woman sniffed. "Not for that pig slop."

None of the grown-ups cared for American food, and they hated the idea of eating in the middle of such dirty work. They preferred to go hungry until they could bathe and eat something decent. But Sundara was ravenous, and as for Ravy, he loved burgers and fries. He ate them every chance he got, and laughed at Soka's warning: "Watch out! You'll start to smell like an American!" Now he slurped down his Coke, dumped the ice, and trotted out to fill the paper cup with wayward golf balls, which he planned to sell.

Grandmother sighed. "I never thought I'd live to see my family work the dirt like peasants."

"Uncle says you loved the garden in Réam."

"A garden is one thing. To slave in someone else's field is another."

"This is hard work, but surely it isn't slavery, Grandmother. We *are* earning money."

"Rubbish! Keeping your knees busy for someone else. How I miss the warm Cambodian sun, my loom in the pleasant shade of the house. Why did they ever force me to come here?"

Sundara did not try to answer. No one could make Naro's mother understand that she was dreaming of a Kampuchea that no longer existed. If she'd stayed behind, she would have seen real slavery. If she'd lived.

"Any day now they'll be locking me in one of those terrible nursing homes."

Sundara sighed. She had heard this so often, it no longer moved her as it had at first. "You know your son will never lock you away, Grandmother. Hasn't he promised?"

"Perhaps a promise doesn't mean the same thing in America. Nothing else does."

Sundara stood, carefully gathering the paper wrappings and stuffing them in the sack. Thank the heavens the season was nearly over. They had begun in June with strawberries and picked every crop in the valley that needed swift and careful human hands for harvest. A whole ton of boysenberries, three tons of pole beans. Sometimes the crops overlapped. One day they had come home exhausted from blueberry picking to find the phone ringing. It was Mr. Bonner. Did they want to pick tomatoes that evening? Wordlessly, they'd piled back into the car.

Tonight they picked until dusk. Their practiced hands could find the little tomatoes with their eyes closed, but they had to quit when they could no longer tell the properly pale orange fruits from the green or overripe red.

Sundara was already at the truck when Soka picked her way, barefoot, out of the tangled rows, weighed down by a stack of three flats. She set them on the wooden pallet with a grunt and straightened up, bracing her back, rubbing her dirty sleeve across her forehead. Strands of black hair had escaped from the knot at the back of her neck and were sticking to her cheeks. She sighed deeply. Then, noticing Sundara watching her, she returned one of those long, searching looks that always made Sundara uneasy.

"What do you think, Niece? Would your mother call me 'little pampered lady' now as she used to?"

Sundara hesitated. Was Soka feeling proud or sad? She answered honestly. "I think not, Younger Aunt."

She busied herself counting the flats and helping Mr. Bonner load them. Fifty for their family. They had done well.

"You people sure can pick," Mr. Bonner said, stacking the last flats on the truck.

"We pick more tomorrow?" Soka asked in her broken but confident English.

Sundara wondered where her aunt found the will to sound so eager for more work when a moment before she seemed ready to collapse.

"Well," Mr. Bonner said, considering, "how about Sunday? My wholesalers won't take anything on Saturday night."

"Okay, Sunday. But first have to go to church." Soka insisted the family present themselves regularly at the First Presbyterian Church, which had sponsored them. "Pray to Buddha, pray to our ancestors, or pray to Jesus Christ," she always said. "It's all the same anyway. The important thing is to go and show our gratitude."

"Do you want to call some of the other families, then?" Mr. Bonner asked.

"Oh, we pick all," Soka put in quickly. "No problem." She knew the words to say to Mr. Bonner. Useful phrases such as "Those other people not pick clean. We pick clean." Or "We happy to start more early in the morning if you want."

"We also wish to pick," said Chun-Ling, the Lam daughter who did most of the interpreting for her family.

"Yes, Lam family, too, of course," Soka said, nodding deferentially at the girl's mother. Sundara and Chun-Ling exchanged glances. Neither had made any effort to become friends, but there was a certain understanding between them. They were, as the Americans put it, in the same boat.

"I guess I'll see *you* tomorrow morning, then, right?" Mr. Bonner said to Sundara.

Sundara nodded, proud. She was the one he'd singled out to sell his produce at the Saturday farmers' market.

They plodded up the parallel ruts of the dirt road, passing through alternating pockets of warm and cool air, wispy puffs of haze forming where the sun-heated earth met the chill of the coming night. Sundara carried Pon in her aching arms, his head nodding sleepily against her shoulder. A few stars blinked, but before they could brighten, the moon loomed above the eastern treetops, glowing orange through the field smoke.

Soka stooped to gather some tender young pigweed she had spotted earlier. She liked to scold Mr. Bonner about all the good food he grew without trying and then never bothered to harvest.

"Listen," she whispered, standing up, holding the greens. "What's that sound?"

They stopped, and in the quiet punctuated only by the chirping crickets, Sundara heard a distant roar. It died away, then rose again, coming from the direction of town. They all looked west, back across the Willamette River, where the lights of town paled the sky.

"I know!" Ravy cried. "It's the high school football game! The fans are going wild!"

"Soka, this son of ours! He's so American."

"I know. How do you think I feel, always having a child explain things to me?" Her voice wavered between annoyance and pride.

"Odd, isn't it?" Naro said. "How the sound carries over the fields."

The football game, Sundara thought. That's probably what the rest of the students were doing tonight. She shifted Pon in her arms and followed the others along the soft dirt road.

CHAPTER 3

The next morning at dawn Sundara pulled the station wagon into the parking lot of Mr. Bonner's produce stand. Gently she shook Ravy awake.

"Time to work, *Ah-own.*" She did not often call him Little Tender One these days, but at this moment it seemed fitting. He looked so small and vulnerable in sleep, breathing softly through parted lips.

He blinked, looked around, and sighed with ten-year-old resignation. "Why do we bother going home at all?"

She smiled. Not a bad question. It had been only a few hours since they left the night before.

"Come. We must hurry."

While Ravy trimmed lettuce, Sundara cut an armload

of pungent dillweed, tying it into bundles. Then she waded into the dewy, overgrown flower patch and went to work with her pocketknife. The sun's rays were shooting over the horizon now, touching the bronze strawflowers and the yellow apples in the orchard with gold.

"Don't forget your wreath," Mr. Bonner reminded her when the big flatbed truck was loaded. He took the circlet of rose-red flowers from its peg in the fruit stand. "Got to keep my reputation. Only farmer down there who's got a princess pushing his stuff."

Sundara smiled, shyly placing it on her head. The first time she'd worn the wreath, Mrs. Bonner had said she looked exactly like an exotic *Sunset Magazine* travel ad: *Come to captivating Tahiti, discover enchantment.* Sundara had blushed, unsure if this was to be taken as a compliment. Then Ravy had elbowed her in that American way he'd learned, and hissed in Khmer, "They think you look pretty, get it?"

Of course. The Bonners always meant to be nice—even if they sometimes said strange things. And Mr. Bonner did seem pleased with her work, had even offered a full-time job all summer if she would work only for him. But Soka and Naro thought the family should work together. "A bundle of chopsticks cannot be broken like one alone," Naro reminded her, and Soka added that even at the piecework rate Sundara might earn more by picking. "Work more hours and help watch little Pon at the same time." Still, the idea of guaranteed work had its appeal. They hadn't forgotten the year the price fell so low on cherry tomatoes that Mr. Bonner couldn't afford to have them picked. Finally they agreed to let Sundara work the Saturday markets. Ravy would be her helper. And, she suspected, her chaperone.

The fir-lined ridges of the Coast Range foothills etched a faint line above the swirling fog as Sundara drove west, back toward town. She hoped the last wisps would burn off quickly; she didn't want to be wearing her shabby jacket when people started coming to the market. But it was still chilly when they pulled into the municipal parking lot by the river. Ravy got out, hopping from one sneakered foot to the other, slapping his thin arms around himself.

"It *is* cold, isn't it?" Sundara said. She envied the Cambodians who had left Oregon for the warmth of southern California. A warmer place might have made her family's exile from Kampuchea less harsh, but they'd had to go where the sponsors could be found. And a sunnier climate alone would not be enough to lure her family away now, not when they finally had a house of their own —a new American subdivision house—and Naro was once again working as an accountant instead of a dishwasher. And at least Oregon was green. Here the luminous, newly sprouted grass fields surrounding Willamette Grove reminded her of the paddies of tender rice shoots covering the lowland Kampuchean countryside. It was good to dwell among living things. She thought of the refugees the resettlement people had sent to the cold gray cities of the northern states. How could they bear it, after the lush green and rich brown of Kampuchea?

"Let's hurry," she said to Ravy now. "You'll feel warmer if we keep moving." They arranged the empty crates as a makeshift counter and tugged the full crates off the truck, struggling to set up ahead of the customers. Already the first eager buyers were poking into the wire-bound crates of corn, asking prices, getting in the way. Sundara quickly filled the bins to give them the overflowing look Mr. Bonner wanted, set out the pails of purple zinnias and spicy pink carnations, then put the raspberries in a tempting spot. It never failed—customers would scurry from all over the lot like ants surrounding sugar to admire and buy the luscious ruby-red fruit.

The bakery lady pulled in next to them, and at the first whiff of warm pastry, Ravy turned his big eyes up at Sundara.

"Oh, all right," she said. "We can split a cinnamon roll." When the first rush of customers passed, she gave him some change. Soka wouldn't like it if she knew. *Save,* she always reminded them. *Don't spend.* But today Sundara could take the money from her own portion, the money Soka allowed her to keep.

She tore off a small piece of Ravy's proffered roll, a bit without the syrupy glaze—too sweet as far as she was concerned. But Ravy had become a real little American, and loved anything with sugar. Sundara watched him gobble his down. He enjoyed it so much, she didn't mind spending the money, but she *did* wish her own savings would add up faster.

She hoped to buy a fine jacket with fleecy lining to keep her warm this winter. This one the church people had given her three years earlier was such an ugly green color, and she was tired of mending the worn-out elastic at the wrists. Now, even though she would have enjoyed the extra warmth a little longer, she pulled it off and put it in the truck cab.

"Ravy, while we're not too busy, why don't you run over and get our eggs?" Soka planned to pickle a jar of them and wanted the brown kind that were harder to find in the stores here. She was still suspicious of these funny white ones.

While Ravy was gone, the mother of the Lam family minced up with her string bag. Sundara touched her palms together in a brief bow.

The Chinese woman picked up a bok choy and regarded it disdainfully. Then she poked a finger at the snow peas. "How much?" she asked in English, the only language she and Sundara had in common. When Sundara told her, she said, "Too much. Not so fresh."

"I promise you, very fresh." Sundara was polite but firm, playing along.

"I give you one dollar a pound."

Sundara clenched her teeth behind her fixed smile. Chun-Ling's mother knew very well she was not free to bargain with Mr. Bonner's produce. The Americans usually preferred to set their prices and stick to them. The woman just liked to make things difficult, Sundara thought, because her own daughter had not been offered this job.

"I am so sorry. I can sell only for the price Mr. Bonner ask."

The woman sniffed indignantly and moved on down the row of parked produce trucks, but Sundara knew she'd be back. No one else at the market today had pea pods or bok choy.

How difficult it was to be pleasant to that dragon of a lady. And Soka always reminding her she ought to be. "Their son would be a good match for you. Look how fast he's educating himself. He already has a job at the computer factory. Of course, it's too bad they are Vietnamese-Chinese instead of Cambodian-Chinese, but still your children would have whiter, prettier skin." Lam Bing would one day be wealthy, Soka confidently predicted. Never mind that his family had been relieved of its gold by Communist Vietnamese officials before boarding that rusting ship. The Chinese, as she said repeatedly, can make money anywhere. "You should be grateful to me, Niece. I'm going to find the very best husband I can for you. You're a pretty girl. Nice and tall. We're not going to give you to just anyone."

But somehow this only made Sundara sad. Her aunt talked as if she'd already lost hope of Sundara's own parents ever coming to take care of these matters. Was Sundara supposed to forget her beloved Chamroeun so easily? Her parents and his had always teased that one day they would be matched in marriage, but it had never been a joke to Sundara. She had loved Chamroeun ever since she was small, from the first time she had peeked down from her perch in the coconut tree and saw him with her older brother, Samet. "If your little sister is so interested in spying on us," he'd said, "why doesn't she climb down and come along to the river?" How she'd loved him for that! What a privilege, to trail behind them through the public gardens! She sighed. Such happy times they'd had, the three of them. . . .

"What are you thinking about *now*?" Ravy asked, coming back with the eggs.

She blinked. "Oh, nothing, Little Brother." Would she ever be free of these memories? The bad ones—the war, the horrible weeks on the ship—came back unbidden, haunting her dreams, flashing on her in unguarded moments; the good ones constantly tempted her with escape. Sometimes it seemed her spirit wanted nothing to do with the present time, the present place. . . .

But soon the customers were forcing her to pay attention. The tomatoes sold quickly, and the ladies in jeans with names on the back pockets were snatching the pretty

LINDA CREW

red pepper strings faster than Sundara could hang them
on the rack. She pulled the last flat of raspberries off the
truck, thinking how happy Mr. Bonner would be with her
load of empty boxes and thick bundle of twenty-dollar
bills.

Then she saw him, the blond boy she'd first noticed in
English class, the one who'd written the funny paper
about cafeteria food. He was pushing his bicycle straight
toward her display.

"Hi," he said.

She gave him a restrained nod. Yes, the same boy. In
class she watched only the teacher or her notes; she had
never looked at him so closely before. Those blue eyes!
She still wasn't used to all the different colorings Americans had. But she liked this boy's blondness. He was not
like the white-haired ones with the pink skins. His skin
was a light brown color, his wavy hair a rich, burnished
gold.

She braced the edge of the flat on the counter, setting
out the pint boxes. Why was her hand shaking so?

"You know, about your poem . . ."

The flat slipped. Luckily she caught it, but heaven protect her—ten dollars' worth of fruit almost turned to jam
on the gravel . . . Her face flamed. That foolish poem.
Whatever had possessed her?

A new rush of customers descended on the stand, forcing him aside.

Sundara fumbled with sacks, had trouble calculating
totals, dropped a slippery head of lettuce. She kept glancing at Ravy to see if he was noticing her odd behavior. But
if she didn't hurry, the blond boy might grow impatient
and leave. And now, somehow, she didn't want him to.

]28[

"You're good at this," he said, after she'd finished with the last tomato customer.

She smiled. "We Khmer women know how to handle money."

He was grinning at her. "To say nothing of big trucks. You really drive this thing?"

She nodded. "Not too hard. Just like a car."

"Sundara. That's your name, right? I'm Jonathan Mc-Kinnon."

"Jonatan." He smiled at her pronunciation. "Hard one for me to say," she explained. "I cannot make the *t-h* sound very well."

"I don't mind."

She fussed with the display, picking off a less than perfect raspberry, adding another cucumber to the box. All the while she eyed him from beneath her lashes. He wore a T-shirt and gray shorts. His thighs were tan and smoothly muscled, covered with curling blond hairs. Embarrassed to be noticing, she glanced away.

"I guess I want some flowers," he finally said.

"Okay." Now she could justify giving him her attention. "Fresh or dried?"

"Uhh . . ." He broke into a grin, shrugging. "Whatever. Which is best, do you think?"

She glanced at Ravy again. He knew perfectly well she wasn't supposed to talk to boys. Hadn't he heard Soka say it often enough? Strange. That rule never bothered her before. It had been her protection against loud, overly bold American boys, made it easier to smile away their advances. But now, somehow, looking at Jonathan McKinnon, she felt constrained by Soka's admonition. They were discussing flowers, yes, but the way he was drawing it all out . . .

She spoke politely, nothing more than a helpful shop-girl. "What you are going to do with the flowers?"

Jonathan simply looked at her, half smiling. After a moment she began to think he'd forgotten to answer.

"Do you like for a gift?" she prodded gently.

He blinked, startled. "Uh, yeah. Right. I'm going to . . . uh. . . ." He brightened. ". . . give them to a girl." Then, inexplicably, he turned red.

These poor Americans with their light skins. How easily they colored with every emotion. No wonder they never seemed to remain properly composed.

Jonathan coughed and hastily pointed to her bushel basket of dried flowers, reading the sign. " 'Everlastings.' Do they really last forever?"

She tilted her head. "Nothing last forever. But last a long time." She smiled, showing her dimples. "Long enough."

"Okay, how about you choosing one for me?"

She gave him a slight, I-am-your-obedient-servant nod. Her hands hesitated over the tissue-wrapped bouquets. Then she plucked one out.

"This is okay?"

"Perfect," he said, looking at her, not the bouquet. Was it possible? Could he actually be flirting? It seemed so, but with Americans it was hard to be certain. . . . He paid; she made change. He pocketed it without counting. So difficult not to stare at his hair, his eyes the color of the sky! Odd, but he made her think of Chamroeun. Here was a boy as golden as Chamroeun had been dark, yet something in the slow warmth of his smile was the same, and curiously familiar.

"Have you decided which trouble spot to do your report on for international relations?" he asked.

"I'm not sure yet." He'd noticed, then, that she was in his honors social studies class.

"I guess I just assumed you'd want to do Cambodia."

"Oh . . ." She looked over to a break in the cotton-woods where the shaded green river slid by. "I don't know . . . Sometime kind of hard for me to think about that."

"Maybe I'll do it, then." He spun the bike pedal with the toe of his dirty running shoe. "Didn't that kill you when the kid at the end of the row was worried there wouldn't be enough trouble spots to go around? We should be so lucky."

"Hey," Ravy piped up. "Do you play golf? I have some good golf balls to sell. Excellent condition and a very fair price."

Sundara and Jonathan exchanged smiles.

"Sorry, I don't play."

"How about your father?"

"Yeah, he does, once in a while."

"Here's my card." Ravy pulled out a baseball card with his name and phone number printed across the back in felt pen.

" 'Ravy's Pre-owned Golf Balls,' " Jonathan read.

"Here's a sample of my quality." Ravy produced a clean white ball from a shoe box stashed under the crate counter.

To Ravy's grinning satisfaction, Jonathan bought a sackful. Then he turned to Sundara. "You know, I was really hoping you'd be here today."

Her cheeks burned. Ravy shouldn't hear this.

"I saw you here last week. I go, 'Who's that?' but I don't usually just walk up and start talking to girls I haven't met." He looked down, spun the pedal again. "I couldn't believe it when you turned up in my English class. And like I said, that poem—it really got to me."

"Ohhh . . ." She looked away toward the river again. "That kind of bad, I write that."

"What do you mean? You made us understand what you feel. That was the idea, wasn't it?"

She sighed. "Maybe everything a person feel should not be told to the world. You have the right idea, I think. Just make everyone laugh."

"But the assignment was to write about something really important to us, right? After I heard yours, I felt like a total turkey, griping about cafeteria food."

She smiled, pleased in spite of her protests. For a moment neither said anything. Catching a whiff of smoke, she turned to watch a brown column rising from across the river. These violent-looking billows had frightened her before she'd heard about field-burning. Now she understood they had nothing to do with war.

Jonathan was tossing and catching one of the golf balls. "So how long have you been in America?" he finally asked.

"We come in 1975."

"Four years? You must have known English before then, right?"

She shook her head. "Only French."

"You speak French?" He sounded impressed.

"*Mais oui!*" She smiled, showing him her dimples again. "Everybody learn French at school in my country, because before the American, we have the French, you see. Too bad we never know we come here, or I would study English instead!"

"So how *did* you learn?"

"Listen a lot. Watch TV. Not much choice. Cannot talk is like a prison. Cannot make a new life."

"And how'd you learn to drive a big truck like this?"

"Same thing as learn English. We come here, we see right away, everybody have to drive. My family make me learn quick, as soon as I'm old enough."

He looked at her for a moment, as if thinking. "Well, I'd better keep moving." He clutched the flowers and the sack of golf balls to his handlebars and pushed off.

"Good-bye," she said, and when he flashed that smile back at her, she added boldly, "See you at school."

She glanced at Ravy. Would he mention this at home? What fate! Having to concern herself with her conduct in front of a ten-year-old boy. But then he gave her a sly smile, which was somehow reassuring. He wouldn't want to betray her, she decided. Not after all they'd been through together.

She looked up and watched Jonathan round the curve of the bike path in a drift of the first-fallen honey locust leaves, his golden hair lit by the sun.

CHAPTER 4

The urgent thump of the pep band vibrated through the crisp night air, drawing the streams of people on the sidewalks toward the football field. Sundara's pulse quickened as she and Ravy neared the bright lights. She was actually going to a football game! Through the chain link fence she caught a glimpse of the field, the growing crowd. They bought their tickets and jostled through the turnstiles.

"Where shall we sit?" she asked Ravy when they were inside.

"Sit wherever you want. I'm meeting my friends over there."

"But Ravy—"

]34[

Too late. He was already headed for a crowd of younger kids in the end zone.

For a panicky moment Sundara thought of leaving. She'd looked forward to the game; she hadn't planned on being alone. But she'd have to stay. Ravy would need a ride home, and that had been the only reason Soka allowed her to come. Taking a deep breath, she went over to the stands. Most of the seats were filled, and to find an empty one a person had to walk along in front of those rally girls, craning, searching while everyone in the stands looked down and thought, Who is that person in the horrid green jacket?

"Sundara! Up here!" It was Kelly, waving her to a seat.

Sundara climbed the wooden steps and nodded gratefully at Kelly's friends as they scooted down to make room for her. A couple of them even smiled and called her by name.

"I can't believe it!" Kelly said. "I never thought I'd see *you* at a *football game.*"

"I can't believe either." Never before had she asked permission to come, and perhaps Soka *had* looked at her a bit suspiciously. But it was a natural thing to want to go to the football game like everyone else, wasn't it?

Sundara could hardly admit even to herself her real interest tonight: Jonathan McKinnon. What did he do in this game that made the girls whisper and giggle when he passed in the hall? She wanted to see for herself.

There were other people she was curious about too.

"Kelly," she whispered after a while, "who is the rally squad girl on the end? To the right?"

Kelly wrinkled her nose. "Oh, that's Cathy Gates. Don't tell me you didn't know that."

Actually, Sundara did know that, but she wanted to

know more. For this was the girl who clung so brazenly to Jonathan in the halls. As Sundara watched, Cathy waved to someone up in the stands and did a perky little dance step that made her breasts bounce under her orange sweater.

"She and Jonathan McKinnon have been going together forever. You know the guy I mean? He's on the team?"

Sundara nodded.

"They went to my junior high. They've always been like this perfect couple. He's really nice. Not stuck-up at all considering he's a big star. Don't you think he's good-looking?"

Sundara nodded again, careful not to show the slightest enthusiasm.

"She's nice, too, I guess. Sometimes it gets kind of sickening, though, all the attention she gets—awards and stuff. I mean, she's not dumb."

Sundara remembered Cathy's English class paper that first week. It was written well enough. Something about the importance of being yourself. But how puzzling. Who else could you be?

Now Sundara's eyes widened as Cathy and the other rally girls launched into a shimmying, hip-wiggling dance.

"Oh, Kelly," she breathed. "I'm shock!"

"What? Oh, I know. Except for the pleated skirts, they could be a bunch of strippers."

Sundara had seen this on television, the young women in the white cowboy hats and the skimpy fringed vests, but these were girls her own age, girls who walked the halls of Willamette Grove High every day!

She watched Cathy Gates swinging her hips, flipping her little skirt up, showing off her thighs. This was what

Jonathan McKinnon liked? She sighed. Perhaps she'd been mistaken in thinking he meant to flirt with her at the market. And yet all week it seemed he'd been trying to play eye games with her in class, staring at her so that she'd look. Of course she wouldn't. She'd been taught to sit erect, face forward. But why would Jonathan McKinnon want to look at her anyway? She was not like Cathy Gates at all.

The players gathered at the sidelines now, hands on their hips. Those funny tight pants! Sundara had to smile behind her hand at the lumpy padding on their thighs. The players didn't seem embarrassed to be dressed this way, though. They strutted around as if they felt quite manly and powerful.

Suddenly they all took off their helmets, dropped to one knee, and put their heads down. The crowd hushed.

"What are they doing?" Sundara whispered to Kelly.

"Praying."

"Praying? What for?"

"To win the game, I guess. Or to do their best. I don't know. Coach Hackenbruck always makes them do it."

The rally girls, too, had their heads bowed.

Sundara frowned. "I thought in this country no one can make you pray."

"Well, people don't argue with Hackenbruck. That's him, there." She pointed out a solidly built man in gray slacks, a V-neck sweater, and a baseball cap.

After the prayer the players stood in a huddle and chanted, "War! War! War! War! Warriors!" Then they ran onto the field.

The band started playing "The Star-Spangled Banner." Sundara stood with the others. Behind her, a boy began singing in a silly falsetto. Sundara turned and eyed him coolly. So disrespectful. Naro would be outraged at this. He always became emotional during the national anthem, especially the part about the land of the free and the home of the brave.

Soon the players were smashing into each other, the men in the striped shirts were blowing whistles and tossing handkerchiefs. Unfortunately, the strange game didn't seem any clearer to Sundara here than it did on television. There must be more to it than she understood. Otherwise, why would the Americans get so excited? At school the crowds parted in respect when two or three of the players in their letter jackets came swaggering down the middle of the hall. But why were football players such heroes?

And Cathy Gates . . . Sundara found herself staring at the girl. She was fascinated with her face, which looked as if it turned on and off with a switch. One instant she'd be standing there with her hip cocked, one elbow cradled in her other hand as she bit her thumb, watching the players on the field. Then something would happen in the game and—click—her face would light up with a big smile as she whirled to face the crowd, clapping and prancing, her brown hair bouncing. Her skin was dark, Sundara noticed, but it was light skin tanned dark, which seemed to make all the difference to the Americans.

Most of all, Sundara envied Cathy's mystifying knack for knowing when Jonathan and his teammates had done something worth cheering about. She always knew whether to chant "Go! Go! Go!" or "Push 'em back, push 'em back, waaaay back!"

When Sundara tried to get Kelly to explain about these things, Kelly just said the main idea was trying to get the ball to one end of the field or the other. This wasn't much help. Sundara could hardly ever see where the ball was! So frustrating, hearing Jonathan's name over the loudspeaker, yet never being able to tell him from the others.

But finally there came a moment when she did see the football. It was arcing high, and the crowd rose as one in a long, tense moan of anticipation. "Aaaahhh . . ." She saw the orange figure running, arms outstretched.

"Come on, McKinnon!" Kelly yelled.

The ball spiraled downward. Jonathan McKinnon leapt, plucked it in midair, and hit the ground running. A deafening cheer rose as he dashed between the white posts.

Sundara found herself on her feet, jumping and clapping with the crowd. She did not understand the game, but she understood speed, she understood grace. She understood why everyone thought Jonathan McKinnon was wonderful.

CHAPTER 5

Standing in the hall after international relations, Sundara's heart pounded so hard she feared Jonathan would hear it. "I don't know much about the politic," she said. "Only what I hear my family say."

"You've gotta know more than I do, though. Come on, let me interview you for my project. It won't take long."

Why did she feel so quivery? Wasn't this just the sort of thing she'd hoped would happen? And it did seem innocent enough. After all, he *was* studying the situation in her homeland for his report; he had the news magazines right there on top of his notebook to prove it.

"Well," she said, "okay. If I can help you." By the time she realized they were going to be conducting this discussion over lunch trays, alone together out on the patio, it was too late to demur. Couples sat together under every tree, on each likely bench; how could she explain, without giving offense, that for her this was wrong?

As he started in on his sloppy joe, she smiled shyly, not meeting his eyes. "Before you tell me your question, can I ask one to you?"

"Sure."

"Ever since I hear your name, I'm wondering. Is your father a doctor?"

"Yeah, a pediatrician."

"Ahh . . . I'm glad." Even though Jonathan looked as though he could be the son of the Dr. McKinnon she remembered, she had thought it unlikely. Would the son of a well-to-do doctor wear such faded jeans, sweatshirts with ragged cut sleeves? In America—yes. "Your father the one take care my cousin when we first come here."

"Yeah?"

She nodded. "Little Pon so sick. Only fifteen pound he weigh at almost two year old!"

"Fifteen pounds." He poked a straw in his milk carton. "Are you sure? My mom says I weighed almost ten when I was born."

"But true. All his meat is gone. Nothing but bone left. We are scared because he is so bad and we cannot understand any English. But your father, he is a very kind man, so tender to all the little one. He make our Pon well again. My aunt say, 'Oh, if the people here are like Dr. McKinnon, maybe America gonna be a good place after all!' This why I'm wondering if you are the son. You see, it is because of your father I am inspired to be a doctor myself."

"You've already made up your mind?"

She nodded. "Before, I think I just take care my chil-

dren when I grow up, cook and like that. But now everything so different. My family want me to be a doctor so I
can go back someday and help my people. They will
need more doctor, because the Khmer Rouge kill all the
old one."

"Oh. Well, I'm impressed."

She was talking too much, she realized suddenly, embarrassed. She should encourage him to speak instead.
"What do *you* plan to be?"

He shrugged. "I don't really know."

"My cousin Ravy—the one you see at the market?—he
is asking me do you plan to be a professional football
player?"

"Don't think so."

"But you are the big star. I see you win the game."

He looked up. "You were there?"

She nodded, glad that at least she'd understood he'd
done something remarkable. "I think football is the most
important American game, right?"

"Well, maybe. But I don't take it as seriously as they
want me to. Mostly I just like to run."

"You very fast."

"Who wouldn't be? You notice the size of some of
those meats chasing me?"

Sundara's hand went to cover her smile. "You all look
big in those funny suits!"

"Yeah, well, those guys *feel* big, too, when they land on
you. Someday I'll probably get clobbered."

"Oh," she breathed, "I hope not." Then she glanced
away. She had no business making it sound as if it mattered so much to her. Even if it did. She cleared her throat
and folded her hands in her lap. "What you want me to
tell you about my country?"

Children of the River

A slow smile spread over his face, a smile that made her go warm all over.

"Right," he said. "This *is* supposed to be business, isn't it? Well . . . let's see . . ." He opened his notebook, flipped through the pages to some jotted questions. "Okay . . . what was it like, living in the middle of a war?"

"Oohh . . . Hard to say. I cannot remember my country without a war. But when I'm small in Phnom Penh, it seem far away. The grown-up keep talking how something bad gonna happen, but I don't pay any attention. By the end, though, no one can ignore. My school close down because of the bombing just when I supposed to take my examination for the *lycée,* and—"

"*Lycée?*"

"Oh, that French. It mean like a high school. Anyway, I study so hard for the test. In my country, you not pass this, no more school for you unless you are a high-up person and your father can pay for private school. My father cannot pay, but he want me to get a good education, so I study hard. Then they shoot the rockets and I don't get to take my test! I get so mad! After that is the long vacation. But all the road into Phnom Penh are blocked so we cannot go down to the sea at Réam. Cannot go anywhere. Cannot even go to the cinema. Just stay home and listen to my mother complaining how the food cost more every time she go to the market. It's like crazy inflation, you know?"

"But you never really saw any fighting?"

She smiled grimly. "Only in our house." She touched her fingers to her lips. "But I shouldn't tell about that." She took a small bite of her sandwich. Surprising, the way the words were pouring out. English words. This American boy had done nothing but smile at her encouragingly and here she was, putting into English things she'd never spoken of before in any language.

"Why shouldn't you talk about it?" Jonathan persisted.

She frowned. "Not right to tell our family trouble . . ." He seemed to be waiting for her to go on. She hesitated, then recklessly plunged ahead. "Just that everybody get so cranky, you know? My father a teacher at another *lycée*, so he home all the time. This the hot season. Everybody kind of pick on each other . . . I'm sorry now. I feel bad when I think how I talk to them."

Jonathan smiled. "Somehow it's hard for me to picture you as a rotten kid."

"It is true. My mother say I'm sassy." She tilted her head. "I'm a different person now, though. Like I already die and now I am reborn."

Jonathan gave her a startled look. She flushed.

Perhaps this was the danger, she thought, in talking to Americans. You constantly risked stepping over some invisible boundary, saying something they'd find odd. As she turned away, she noticed a group of boys lounging around the picnic tables, gawking at them.

"They think it funny, you talking to me."

Jonathan turned. "Oh, that's just a bunch of guys from the team. They like to give me a hard time."

Most of them were much bigger than Jonathan, Sundara noticed. Wider. They looked mean, with their tight T-shirts and muscles.

"Hey, McKinnon!" one yelled. "We vote nine!"

Jonathan tried to wave them off.

"What does that mean?" Sundara asked. " 'We vote nine'?"

He shook his head. "Nothing. It's stupid."

"Please? I want to know."

"Oh, it's just this dumb thing they're into lately—rating girls. You know that movie *10*?"

Sundara shook her head. "We never go to movie here."

One of the boys yelled, "Ten if she wears a grass skirt!"

Jonathan's face turned red. He shook his head. "Just ignore them." He laced his fingers behind his head and leaned back against the cement bench, stretching out his legs. "They're right about one thing, though. You would look great in a grass skirt."

"A grass skirt?"

"You know, like one of those South Sea Island girls. Tahitians or whatever. That's what I thought the first time I saw you."

She glanced away, flustered. He *was* flirting. Unless she was absolutely hopeless at interpreting American boys. . . . But no—somehow she felt sure the look on his face was the same in any language.

"Khmer women don't wear grass skirts," she said, thinking even as she spoke what a stupid remark this was. But how could she be clever when he was making her so nervous?

He shrugged, gave her that slow smile again. "You look great in jeans too."

Absolutely shameless, that's what he was! She cocked her head at him. "This is part of the interview?"

"Oops. Sorry." He sat up straight. "I'll try to be good."

While he made a show of studying his questions, she was thinking about her jeans. Soka always complained they were too tight. Maybe they were. She smiled to herself.

"Okay . . ." Jonathan looked up. "Do you think it's

possible that people watching war coverage on TV see more bombing and stuff than the people actually there do?"

She blinked at the change of subject. "I don't know. We don't have a TV in Cambodia. Do they show a lot of bomb?"

"Here, they did," Jonathan said. "Every night."

"What I see," she told him, "is what the war does to the people. Before, Phnom Penh is a beautiful city, but by the end it's crowded with refugees from the countryside. You know, they make a tent on all the sidewalk . . ." She trailed off. Sitting here in the peaceful autumn sunshine, all that seemed so long ago and far away. Did she really want to bring it back? The wretched women fanning clouds of flies from their sick-looking children. The stench of overflowing garbage rotting in the late dry-season heat. You couldn't get that from television. The cratered streets, the rubbled buildings, the people with limbs missing, wounds bound in filthy bandages, crusty with rust-red blood . . .

"The main thing I remember about the Vietnam War," Jonathan said, "is my mother's antiwar petitions. She and my dad got in a big fight because one time she took them to a party for people from the clinic. My dad had just started working there and he was afraid people would get upset."

"And did they?"

"It upset my dad, that's for sure." Jonathan shrugged. "So that's my memory of the war. I didn't really understand what it was all about; I just knew it was something so horrible, Mom had to keep turning the TV off so I wouldn't see it on the news."

Sundara sighed. "My mother doesn't want me to see it

either. That's why they keep me home. I never know how bad everything is until I leave."

"I'll bet you're glad you got out when you did, huh?"

She felt the corners of her mouth twitch. Jonathan saw this.

"Look, we don't have to talk about Cambodia, if it's going to make you feel bad."

"I don't mind, if it help you for your report."

"Well, if you're sure." He tapped the *Newsweek* on the top of his stack. "I've already read some about it. Enough to know I'm really glad you got out of there. I mean, I know you miss your home, but from what I've read about the Khmer Rouge being so down on intellectuals, it would have been terrible if you'd stayed. Your dad a teacher . . ." He shook his head. "Just lucky he got out in time."

"But Jonatan . . ." She laid down her fork carefully. "He doesn't get out."

Jonathan's sloppy joe stopped halfway to his mouth. "What do you mean? I thought—"

"I leave my whole family in Phnom Penh."

He dropped the sandwich onto the tray. "Oh, God, Sundara. I'm *sorry*. I didn't know. When you talked about your family I just assumed . . ."

"No, I come with my aunt and uncle because I'm with them in Réam when Phnom Penh fall down. Maybe I don't explain right before."

He swallowed hard. "So what happened to your parents?"

"I don't know. I hear nothing."

"In all this time?"

She shook her head. "The last day I see my father is when he take me to the airport."

"But that's awful."

She nodded. "My parent send me on the plane to Réam only a couple week before the Khmer Rouge take over. Plane is the only way out because all the road blocked. That's when I see the city all falling apart. The boulevard jam full of bicycle, oxcart, motorcycle, big green soldier truck—everything. All the big, pretty house pile up with sandbag to protect. I just hang on to my father in the pedicab and stare. I never know until now how bad the war is making everything. I remember the driver drop us at the taxi station, says, 'Twenty riel.' My father say, 'You crazy! That four time the regular.' He go, 'This war. You not the only one in a hurry to get someplace.' The airport a mess too. Everybody pushing, worried to get out. Then the shell come screaming."

"Right when you were there?"

"Yes! My father throw me on the pavement. My chest burn, I'm so scared. I feel the hot ground shake my face. Then he yank me up, drag me to the plane step. By now I don't want to go at all, just want to stay with my family. I'm crying, but he doesn't listen. I tell him, look, my elbow bleeding and his glasses have a crack, but he just shove me up with the people."

"And you haven't heard anything since then?"

"No. Only the rumor about what happen when the Khmer Rouge take Phnom Penh. A few who escape say the Communist make everyone march into the country to work and many die. Sometime I say to myself, 'Sundara, you may already be *kamprea*.' That mean orphan. A couple day ago we have a holiday, All Soul Day. We pray for everyone who already die. But I don't know who to pray for, because—well, who die and who doesn't?"

After a moment Jonathan shook his head as if he couldn't believe her story. "Leaving without your parents . . ." he said.

"*And* my brother and little sister." She sighed. "And Chamroeun."

"Chamroeun?"

"He a boy I know."

"Boyfriend?"

She studied her hands. "Kind of like that." She looked up at him again. "Maybe I shouldn't make you sad about this."

For a long time they said nothing. They had both stopped eating. Finally she said, "How many brother and sister do you have?"

"None. I'm it."

"Ah! That too bad!"

He blinked. "There *are* certain advantages to being an only child, you know."

"Oh, forgive? I don't meaning to offend."

"No, that's okay." He laughed. "I guess I'm just not used to people feeling sorry for me. Everybody always acts like I'm the kid with everything."

"But no brother or sister . . ."

He shrugged. "I'm used to it."

"Oh." She glanced away. "In Cambodia we like to have many children. Five is good. If you can support a lot of children and they healthy, you feel rich."

Jonathan frowned. "Actually, I think my parents did want more kids. I didn't understand what was going on at the time, but I'm pretty sure my mom had a bunch of miscarriages."

"Miscarriage?"

LINDA CREW

"You know, babies that didn't make it. Babies that were never born."

"Oh. Very sad."

They were quiet for a moment, then she spoke again.

"I have a lot of fun with my brother and sister, even if I act mad with them sometime. Samet have more freedom because he's a boy, and Mayoury, she the little one, so naturally she kind of get spoiled. But I'm just the middle daughter. So when my mother say she sending me to Réam, I say, 'Good, I be glad to get away.' But then I get homesick. You see how foolish? I have to go away before I see how I love my family."

"I guess that's the way it is with a lot of people. You know: Absence makes the heart grow fonder."

"Yes! That *exactly* how it is. The American understand this too, then!" She repeated it. "Absent make the heart grow fonder." She sighed. "That so true!"

"Look," he said, "if it's bothering you to talk about all this . . ."

She laughed shortly. "I say we shouldn't talk about, then I start again."

"You don't have to. Maybe I shouldn't have brought it up at all."

"No, that's okay. You know, I never talk about this before. Not to an American."

"Really?"

She nodded. "I don't mind telling, if you sure you want to hear."

"I do. Go on. How did you get out of Cambodia?"

She took a deep breath. "Well, my uncle is like a clerk for the U.S. government, and if the Communist get him that not gonna be good. . . ." She drew a finger across her throat. "So when we hear they coming we run down and get on the ship. Everybody say, 'Oh, we just stay away a couple day, let everything settle down.' But pretty soon some people come by in a little boat and say already they are killing. So we leave."

"And headed for America," Jonathan said thoughtfully.

"Oh, we not heading *for* anyplace. We just getting away from the killing. First we go Thailand, then Malaysia, Indonesia . . . We don't know *where* we gonna end up. We just floating around like that for six, seven week. Finally the American let us come to a camp in the Philippine. We stay there awhile, then they bring us to California."

"I was asking my folks about this and they seemed to think everybody who left Vietnam and Cambodia in '75 was evacuated by our government. All nice and orderly, like it was planned ahead of time."

"No." She shook her head. "Nobody ever talk about leave Cambodia, not to me. My aunt and uncle never talk about 'Let's pack' or 'Better get ready.' Just pick up and go that day." She sighed. "I don't want to go. I want to go back to Phnom Penh because I'm so scared for my family, but my uncle say, 'Niece, no time to cry! Too late! Come on!' "

She paused. "Why you look at me that way?"

He shook his head. "God, I can't imagine having to leave my home like that, then try to go on with my life in some other country without knowing what had happened to my family."

"But as long as I don't hear they die, I still have hope." She made her voice light. "I know a Korean girl—her mother just find her sister again, almost thirty year since the war in Korea. Me, I'm only hoping four year so far!"

But Jonathan just stared at the ground.

Sundara bit her lip. Perhaps they should have stuck to the subject of grass skirts after all.

CHAPTER 6

Of all the guests seated on their living room floor Sunday evening, Sundara was happiest to see her friend Moni.

"How lucky I feel," the round-faced older girl was saying now, "to sit down to your good food, Soka." Every time Moni came over she seemed a little plumper. "I don't care how fat I get," she had often told Sundara. After eating insects, rats, and scorpions to stay alive, a few extra pounds seemed like a smart idea.

Soka urged another plateful on her. "It helps, being able to glean for the garlic. When it's free, I don't have to be stingy with it. As for the rice, I just have to do the best I can with the pitiful stuff they sell here."

Grandmother sighed. "How I miss the rice we had at

home, the way it always smelled so fresh. The kind we get here has all the goodness milled right out of it."

"I'm just thankful they have rice at all in America," Moni said. "I'm such a lobster brain, I had the notion they ate only bread!"

Sundara joined in the soft laughter. She liked the way Moni was never afraid to tell a joke on herself. After everything she'd been through, it was surprising she could laugh at all.

Back in Cambodia, Moni's young husband had been a soldier. Left alone while he fought the Communists, she'd taken refuge in Phnom Penh to await the birth of her baby —one among thousands, camping on the sidewalks. When the Khmer Rouge took the city, she, like many others, hoped for the best. Maybe the Communists would not be so bad. At least the fighting and killing would stop. And soon she could be with her husband again. For a brief hour or so as the truckloads of soldiers rumbled through the streets, people actually cheered.

But the mood of celebration did not last. Soon the soldiers were ordering everyone to leave the city. The Americans, they said, were coming in their B-52s to bomb Phnom Penh. Easy to believe. Hadn't the American search for lurking North Vietnamese already cratered much of the Cambodian countryside?

As the march from Phnom Penh began, Moni's time came, as the Khmer women say, to swim the Great River. On a sidewalk, with people trudging past, she gave birth. Soka and Sundara had wept to hear this, but Moni assured them she was not the only one. "And much worse things were happening. After my baby was born, a little boy begged me for help. He must have been one of those thrown out of the hospital because his foot . . . was gone.

But I couldn't carry him. I was so weak myself and with my own new baby . . . Oiee, his little spirit comes to me still."

Naturally, Soka and Sundara assumed her baby had died; many Khmer babies failed to survive under much better conditions. Soka herself had lost two between Ravy and Pon. But Moni said no, she lived. "She was a strong little peasant, like me."

Not knowing which direction to walk, the city dwellers had been herded around the countryside by the dead-eyed, black-garbed soldiers. But Moni plodded steadily north toward her parents' rice-farming village, baby tied in her *krama*. She ate whatever she could find, even tree bark, when she came across some that was free of the Americans' leaf-killing poison spray. At her parents' she recovered, but soon learned her husband would have been one of the first executed when the Khmer Rouge began their purge. And the new Kampuchea had no place for the widows of anti-Communist soldiers. She, too, was marked for death.

Leaving the baby with her parents, she fled on foot, her breasts aching with the milk her baby would never suck. Through the jungle she made her way, braving wild panthers and Khmer Rouge soldiers, picking around the mines and the scattered bones of those who'd chosen the wrong place to step. She'd even managed to sneak past the thieves at the Thai border.

Her story haunted Sundara. Such courage. Not only had Moni given birth to the child, but she kept it alive. How had Moni succeeded in this, where Sundara had failed? But Sundara's guilt about Soka's baby was something she could never discuss. Not even with Moni.

Now she rose and stepped carefully through the seated

crowd. Since the small dining area could not hold all the guests, Naro, Soka, and Sundara had pushed back their few pieces of furniture and spread mats over the wall-to-wall carpeting in the living room. It was often like this, because their friends liked to put on the *sampot*s and sarongs they did not feel comfortable wearing elsewhere and come eat with Naro and Soka in their new, American-style house. People wanted their advice, for they had been in the United States the longest. Sometimes Soka complained privately about the inconvenience, but what could they do? Friends must be made welcome, even the unexpected ones.

Sundara returned from the kitchen with Soka's silver-colored palm leaf plate on which she'd arranged the *karup kanow*, a dessert of candied jackfruit. The children were up now and running around, chasing each other with gleeful shrieks, pausing only to snatch one of the golden morsels. The parents frowned, but not too sternly. *"Kompuch!"* they called after their little ones jokingly. "Such bad manners!"

But Soka assured them she didn't mind the noise. "It makes me happy in my heart to hear them laugh like that after all that's happened."

"You're lucky," one sad-eyed woman said to Soka. "Your children didn't see the terrible things mine did."

Please don't start, Sundara thought to herself, passing the plate. Perhaps it was unkind, but she dreaded the company of this woman. Except for her daughter and herself, Pol Pot's men had killed her entire family. Sundara felt truly sorry for her, but if she started to tell her story one more time, every detail about the horrifying way they'd died . . .

"Your little girl will forget the bad things," Soka said,

also wanting to steer the woman away from repeating her tale. "Look at her now." The child in question raced by, panting with laughter, chasing Pon. She seemed perfectly normal except for one thing: her almost hysterical aversion to wearing any item of red clothing. A reminder of blood.

"I worried about my little Pon for a long time," Soka went on. "I'll never forget when I first had to take him to the day-care center. Both of us crying! I couldn't believe my sponsor expected me to leave him with people who weren't even family. What kind of cruel place is this America? I thought. But I got used to it, and as you can see, he is fine."

Now, under Ravy's direction, the children were making a tent, using the many hand-crocheted afghans given them by the church ladies. A small, grinning face poked out of the colorful tent flap, then disappeared inside.

Sundara smiled, then sighed. Sometimes she wished she were a few years younger. The children did seem happier. Even the small ones from the other families who had survived the worst of it seemed to do well, starting American school so early. Pon, of course, remembered nothing, and if Ravy did, he didn't dwell on it. His mind was full of *Star Wars*, pocket calculators, and organizing another touch football game with his many friends. Oh, sometimes he spoke wistfully of the pet rooster he'd had to leave behind, but for Sundara . . . she almost felt she'd left her whole *self* behind, that laughing girl who had run along the sparkling sand beaches at Réam, made a mischief in the dusty streets of Phnom Penh . . .

Only a few weeks before she'd left the country forever, her father had given her the loveliest blue parasol painted with pink roses—not a good gift, as it turned out, to cheer a girl weary of remaining at home. How she'd pleaded with him to take her walking along the quay. In her mind she saw herself twirling it, drawing the attention of the boys on their bicycles. Of course, in her father's presence, she could hardly return their smiles, but how pleasant to see them watching her. And maybe she and Papa could stop at one of the Parisian-style cafés? Or take a pedicab ride to the Chinese shopping district?

"Innocent One, I cannot take you. It's too dangerous with the rockets. And believe me, the city is not as you remember it."

Hateful war. It ruined everything.

And now, in spite of everything she'd gone through in the months that followed, everything that showed her just how sheltered she'd been and how little she'd understood of the war, this one thought still haunted her: Never would she stroll the Boulevard Monivong beneath the lavender jacarandas and blooming peacock trees, twirling a painted parasol. Not while her hair was still black, anyway, not while she was young and pretty. Shamefully foolish, this regret, but somehow she couldn't get rid of it.

"Some of the older children surprise me with their American ways too," the wife of Prom Kea was saying now. "Did you hear about Pok Simo, the son of Pok Sary? His American friends taught him to play poker and he won all their money from them!"

Sundara frowned to herself. Pok Simo was just a year ahead of her in school. She didn't like him. Why did the others find his poker playing so admirable? Because he'd beaten the Americans? Even Soka smiled. It made little sense. Sundara could just imagine the trouble if Soka learned *she'd* been gambling—at any time other than the

New Year, that is. Then it was permitted. But this was different. Pok Simo was making a career of it.

"Yes, he's a smart boy. They say he is already planning to take military training in college."

Naro scoffed. "What's so smart about going into the military? If your country is defeated, what are you going to do for a job?"

Now the talk turned, as it always must, to the problems of life in America. Why did they have to pay those social security taxes? Wasn't that what families were for? But smuggling money back to the ones at home, that was a problem too. They always wanted more. They thought America was heaven because everyone had a car. They didn't understand that everyone *had* to have a car. And speaking of cars, wasn't it terrible the looks they got for driving shiny new ones? They'd saved and paid cash, hadn't they? And bought American, too, not Japanese! There was no way to win. If they went on welfare, Americans called them spongers. If they worked hard and succeeded, people got jealous.

Among the guests were a man and wife newly arrived in America, and they listened, wide-eyed, as the others went on and on, saying the same things Sundara had heard so many times before. How strange all this must sound to them, she thought. Only a few weeks ago they'd been languishing in a squalid refugee camp, probably imagining America as the answer to every prayer.

Then again, Sundara thought, at least they'd been *wanting* to come here. Waiting, they'd had time to get used to the idea.

For her family, it had all happened with such bewildering speed. She had not known she was leaving her home, perhaps forever, that frantic April night when they boarded the ship. Not until two months later had it dawned on her this was not some temporary sojourn, a terrible but brief interlude until the trouble at home blew over. When it hit her, she was sitting in the tent of a hastily assembled orientation class at Camp Pendleton, California. *Heaven protect me,* she'd thought, her eyes glazing with sudden, stunned dismay. The teacher was explaining how to live in America—as if that's what they'd be doing for a long, long time. They were not going home, not soon. Maybe never. Good-bye Kampuchea, hello America. They'd made one conscious decision—to flee for their lives —and here they were. Just yesterday, it seemed, she'd been swinging on a breezy porch in a Cambodian fishing village, now she was sweltering in an armed camp guarded by rifle-toting American soldiers.

Still, Sundara thought now, looking at the newly arrived husband and wife, this family's long, idle months in the Thai camp were nothing to envy, and even with the support of fellow Khmers it would be harder for them in many ways, coming now. They could not have escaped with their savings in a few rubies, sapphires, or leaves of gold as Naro and some of the other first ones had, and no doubt they were already worn down with having suffered so many difficulties. Sundara glanced at the dazed-looking young mother. She felt sympathetic, but hoped the woman would not be the kind to tell every terrible detail over and over.

Her heart sank when she saw Naro going to the tape deck. Not that tape of Khmer music. Not that song about the woman in the refugee camp. Even the tiring complaints about American life were better than dwelling on this sadness.

]60[

Children of the River

When I read the words you wrote
I thought my dying hour had come
You say you've found a new life, a new wife
In a far-off foreign land.

Over the mountains I've led our children
With one fierce hope of finding you
Now they're weeping at my knees, begging please
Won't I tell them where you've gone?

Over the sea I send my spirit
To hurt your heart with one sad plea
Hear them cry for their father, though you love
    another
And have long forgotten me.

Sundara's throat closed. The woman who'd lost her
family broke down and sobbed. Soka moved to comfort
her.

Naro shook his head sadly. "I still cannot understand
how it's come to this: People fleeing not only from the
Vietnamese, but also from fellow Khmers. Our own people! The Vietnamese are not slaughtering each other."

Oh, stop, Sundara thought.

"It seems impossible," the new man offered quietly,
"but many are saying the Vietnamese will be an improve-
ment over the Khmer Rouge."

"What a choice! Like running from the tiger on the
land and being eaten by the alligator in the water. The
Vietnamese would be happy to see every Khmer starve so
they could occupy our country permanently."

"Ah! If only Prince Sihanouk would come back."

They sighed with longing. Once, as a small child, Sun-

dara had been part of the joyful throng that greeted Sihanouk on a wide, tree-lined boulevard in Phnom Penh. Her
memories were not of the beloved ruler, however, but of
the flowers everyone tossed at his slowly passing car, the
necklace of fragrant jasmine she'd been given to wear in
celebration. These older ones remembered Sihanouk himself, though. Somehow they thought if he could return
from exile in China and rule Kampuchea once again, they
might go home.

Why listen to this? Sundara thought, and she rose to
collect the bowls. They might go on with this sighing and
pining all night.

But perhaps the others had had enough too. The
women began gathering in one corner, Soka taking the
new family's baby in her arms. Jennifer was her name.
"She born here!" her father liked to say in English. "She
American!"

"Do you want to give this little one to me to keep?"
Soka joked. "Of course, everyone prefers sons, but a
daughter is good too."

Soka would never have a daughter now. Everyone had
told them it cost thousands of dollars to have a baby in the
United States; where were they going to get money like
that? Soka had felt she had no choice; shortly after arriving, she had the operation for no more babies.

Sundara watched her aunt with a kind of pained fasci-
nation, wondering if she was remembering the baby
daughter that had died.

Soka looked up from Jennifer now. Her black eyes fell
on Sundara and the smile faded. "You can do the dishes,
Niece."

"Yes, Younger Aunt." Sundara slipped into the
kitchen, suddenly trembling. Whenever Soka looked at

her that way, she imagined her aunt saying to herself, *There is the girl who was sent to care for my little child and let her die instead.*

Moni followed with plates balanced on her forearms. "Let me help." Moni always had to be busy, as if to justify her presence. Easy to understand. How else could a girl feel without a real place of her own in a family? And Moni had no family at all, not here. Until recently she'd had to live with her American sponsors. They'd finally been able to help her get her own tiny apartment, but Sundara knew she was lonely.

"The Millers didn't have one of these dishwashing machines," Moni said, "so I still don't understand how to work them."

"It's easy. You scrape and I'll show you how to load it."

Things like this made Sundara feel older than her friend, even though Moni was twenty-two. Having come to America earlier, Sundara understood many things about life here that Moni did not. But in other ways, Moni was the wiser; she knew something of men.

Deftly, Sundara fit the plates in the racks. "Why must they always play those songs?"

Moni shook her head. "That one about the woman and her children could make a stone statue weep."

"And what about the one where the girl is stranded in Long Beach with a new baby because the man she escaped with abandoned her?"

"Ah, that's a sad one too," Moni agreed. "That really happened to a girl I know. And of course her family has disowned her because they never approved of the match in the first place. But sometimes I wonder which is worse—

being abandoned by your husband, or being stuck with one you don't like."

Sundara pondered this as they worked. What a dilemma.

"Remember that girl from Salem?" Moni went on. "The one who's pregnant? She's *miserable*. She confessed to me the other day that she only married her husband because it looked like he had a good chance of being sponsored to America. Now, she says, he's turned mean, he beats her, and she swears she'd rather be back rotting in the refugee camp with the man she loves than here in America. Life here is not at all what she was expecting."

Sundara poured the blue detergent into the cup. "That's not surprising. You'd need a powerful dream to sustain yourself through all that time in the camp. Day after day you'd be promising yourself your troubles would be over if only you could get to America. And then, of course, it doesn't turn out that way." She closed the dishwasher door and punched the start button.

Moni jumped at the rush of water.

Sundara smiled. "Don't worry, it's supposed to sound like that. Now, speaking of men and the troubles they bring, have you seen Chan Seng?"

Moni glanced behind her to make sure they were still alone. "Can you keep a secret? We are thinking of getting married."

"That's wonderful! But why a secret?"

"I'm not blind. I'm not deaf. I know everyone was whispering about me when I danced the *lamthon* with him at New Year's. So bold, they said. A girl who goes wherever the wind blows. They say I should marry that man from Battambang. The one who lives in Portland? Can you imagine? What a feverish rat! He's no man for a strong woman like me. But I like Chan Seng. I think everyone was too hard on him about his arrest. I think he honestly did not understand that in this country you can't go around catching the birds in the parks to eat."

Sundara murmured sympathetically, but she was remembering Naro's anger at this incident. He had called Chan Seng a fool and complained that it made them all look bad. He hated to see that kind of thing get into the newspapers.

"You see, Sundara, since I have no one to arrange a marriage for me, I must do the best I can. I want to make a new life, start a family of my own. How can this happen if I do nothing but wait?"

"But won't everyone be pleased you've found a Khmer to marry?"

"I hope so." There was a hesitancy in Moni's voice, a note of doubt Sundara did not understand. There was nothing in this match that would surprise anyone. They had all seen marriages between refugees agreed upon in as little as two days. Everyone understood that feeling, the impatience to belong to a family again.

"Are you still wondering," Sundara said gently, "if your first husband is alive?"

"Oh, no. Many people saw the soldiers loaded onto the trucks and driven away. None of them ever came back." She bit her lip. "I still think about him, but I am sure he is dead." After a moment she said, "That is past. Life here is so different, I already feel as if I've died myself and been reincarnated."

"Moni! That's exactly how I feel sometimes!"

Moni nodded. "I want to think about the future now."

Later, when all the guests had gone, Sundara retired to her corner of the garage, a space defined by a square of rug remnant, a shelf arrangement of produce boxes, and a suspended plastic pipe where she hung her few clothes. She pulled the string on the bare light bulb and found her chemistry book. Then she curled up on the canvas cot, wrapping herself in the afghan Soka let her use. Colder, these nights. Soon she'd be sleeping in her coat again.

It had been such a long day—church, picking all afternoon, then this gathering. She had not studied as much as she'd meant to, and now she couldn't concentrate.

She kept thinking of Moni. As hard as Moni tried to keep to Khmer ways, people still disapproved of her. It didn't seem fair. Would it be this way for her too?

She decided to speak to her uncle. Somehow, Naro seemed more approachable, less intimidating than her aunt. She went into the dining area where he sat working over more letters on behalf of Soka's sister in the camp.

"Uncle?"

"Yes?"

"You know I am seventeen now." She paused. "Wasn't Soka just seventeen or eighteen when you married her?"

Naro frowned. "You want to get married?"

"Oh, no! I just wondered. . . . Things are so different here. Girls go out with boys . . ."

"Not Khmer girls."

Sundara looked down at the flower-patterned vinyl floor. How could he be so sure the way it would be with Khmer girls in America? Wasn't she herself one of the first faced with growing up here?

"I'm surprised you choose to hurt my ears about this. Don't we have enough problems? Besides, this is something for us to think about, not you. Your aunt and I will see about a husband for you at the proper time."

Children of the River

"Uncle, please pardon my boldness, but Younger Aunt is already talking of matching me with that Chinese boy."

"Well, naturally she wants to keep her eyes open for a good match. If some family offers an especially handsome bride-price . . ." His hand chopped the air. "Enough of this. Medical school is your goal. Your task is to go and study. Mine is to finish these letters."

Sundara hesitated. There was so much more she wished to discuss. Should she explain about Chamroeun to help stall off her aunt's matchmaking? Should she remind her uncle how few suitable Khmer men they actually knew? No, obviously he considered the conversation concluded, so she returned to the garage.

For a moment she just stood there, peering into the far, dark corners, the cold of the smooth cement floor chilling her stockinged feet. Everything was different now. Couldn't he see that? *Everything.* What a long way she was from the airy, tile-roofed house she'd known as a child. At first they'd even been afraid to sleep in these strangely tight American dwellings. There was no air! Surely they would suffocate! Now she was used to it, but still . . .

Padding past the station wagon, her roommate, she checked the locks on the garage door and made sure the curtains they'd rigged over the glass panels were properly closed. Almost every night when she did this, she thought of home, and wished she were latching the shutters of the room she had shared with her sister Mayoury, taking in one last breath of the fragrant frangipani blossoms down in the garden instead of the stink of gasoline and laundry detergent. . . .

But enough of this dangerous dreaming! She had nearly forgotten to put the last load of clothes into the

]67[

dryer. She would not want to face a morning where Soka found wet clothes when she was counting on dry ones.

She climbed back onto her cot to the hum of the dryer, the rhythmic click of Pon's overall buckles against the metal drum. Not so long ago, she reflected, it had seemed quite reasonable that she should marry whoever was chosen for her, especially when the chosen one was Chamroeun. Now, somehow, she felt uneasy about this. What if it couldn't be Chamroeun? What if Soka thought only of the man's income and didn't care if he was kind or had a nice smile? She didn't want to be like the unhappy girl in Salem. And as for Naro's admonition to think only of her education . . . Well, becoming a doctor was so far in the future, and right now, in this lonely time, a chemistry book was no comfort at all. She needed something closer, sooner, something to make her eager for each new day.

But then, she *was* looking forward to something, wasn't she? Or more precisely, someone.

She hugged the afghan tight around her shoulders, alarmed at admitting this, even to herself. Such secret feelings would have to be guarded with utmost care, heaven protect her, for this certain someone was white, he was American, he was absolutely forbidden.

CHAPTER 7

"So—how about it?" Jonathan said. "We could go to the movies if you want. Whatever."

"Oh . . ." She looked away from him, across the patio, stalling for time. A date. He was actually asking her out on a date. A picture flashed in her mind: Jonathan on the doorstep, like in the TV commercials, Naro and Soka looking him over, making him promise to bring her home on time. . . . No, no, never in a thousand years . . . She turned back to Jonathan. "Thank you, but I cannot."

"Come on, don't you like me?"

Her cheeks burned. "You teasing." He knew very well she liked him.

"Sorry." He smiled, not sorry at all. "But what's the problem?"

She bit her lip. "I like to go with you, but—in my country, we don't go out on a date at all."

Still he smiled, refusing to take her seriously. "How do you figure out who you want to marry, then?"

"Our parents arrange. The boy's mother ask the girl's mother."

"But that's . . . *archaic*."

She lifted her chin. "My family would choose well for me. And my mother and father, they very happy together, even they see each other for the first time on their wedding day."

"Yeah?" He sounded skeptical.

She shifted away from him. "If the family make a good match, two people can grow to love each other. Our system not so bad." She gave him a sidelong look. "In Cambodia we do not talk divorce every time somebody get mad."

"Hey, I didn't mean to sound critical. It's just that things are different here."

"Yes," she said, softening, "but not for me."

His smile had faded. He seemed bewildered. "So you really won't go out with me?"

"Jonatan, I shouldn't even have lunch with you. To go to the movie . . . I'm sorry. I just can't."

He blinked, at a loss. "Well . . . I guess if that's the way you feel . . ."

She thought about Cathy, about the other girls who gave him admiring glances. Perhaps no one had ever turned him down before. He looked so hurt.

But was she supposed to throw away the traditions of centuries to save the feelings of one American boy?

Of course not.

Still, imagine . . . to openly say to the world, *Yes, I want to be with him and he wants to be with me.* To venture into public, the two of them, alone together for all to see . . .

No, of course not.

But she couldn't pretend she hadn't felt it—a surprising little thrill of temptation.

After PE one day, Sundara and Kelly were dressing amid clouds of steam and deodorant spray when Cathy Gates started talking about Jonathan on the other side of the lockers.

"Leave it to me," she said, "I'll get him to do the rally skit."

"I wouldn't count on it, Cath. Craig says Jonathan's acting kind of weird lately."

"Well, he's *my* boyfriend," Cathy said. "I ought to know him better than Craig Keltner does."

My boyfriend. Something welled up in Sundara. How easily those words slipped off this girl's tongue.

"What's the matter?" Kelly said.

Sundara had stopped dressing and was standing still, her head tilted. She laid a finger across her lips and glanced toward the lockers.

"I've *told* you," Cathy's voice came again. "He's just working on a class project with her. And the only reason he's doing it at lunch is because he didn't get lunch period with us. Believe me, it's nothing."

Nothing. Had Jonathan actually said that?

Kelly leaned close to Sundara. "Are they talking about you?"

Sundara nodded grimly. Perhaps it was as Soka said. There was an order to things. Family must come first. Blood lines must not be broken. Destroy the order and it will destroy you. She'd opened her heart just the tiniest bit to an American boy, and already this had given Cathy's words the power to tear her apart. She resumed buttoning her blouse.

Cathy's friend said something Sundara couldn't catch. Then Cathy laughed in that easy, confident way she had. Sundara flushed. Maybe she *was* just a class project to Jonathan. She hadn't thought so, especially when he asked her out. But what did she understand about American boys? As Cathy said, he was her boyfriend. She was the one who really knew him.

Cathy and her friend slammed their lockers and left.

"What's going on?" Kelly asked.

Sundara clicked the padlock on her gym basket. "Jonatan McKinnon. Her boyfriend, but he ask me to have lunch with him every day."

"So that's where you've been!" Kelly stared in awe. Then she bounced up from the bench. "Well, does he like you, or what? This is really incredible!"

Sundara raised her eyebrows. "This is such a shock, that he can like me?"

"No, no, I didn't mean it that way. It's just that . . . Jonathan McKinnon! If he ever even looked at me I'd probably melt into a helpless little puddle. And he *likes* you?" She peered at Sundara, trying to push her glasses up by wrinkling her nose. "I don't get it. You just do not look the way a normal, sane girl ought to look if Jonathan McKinnon likes her!"

"Oh, Kelly, not so simple for me. Better he doesn't like me. I'm so scared. My family hear about this, they gonna be mad."

"Who cares?" Kelly said. "For a boy like him I'd let my parents completely disown me."

Children of the River

Sundara had to smile. Kelly was so funny. But she
could afford to talk this way; for her, being thrown out
wasn't a real possibility.

"So what's he really like?" Kelly wiggled her eyebrows. "Up close and personal? I mean, what do you guys
talk about?"

"Well, he want to know about my life in Cambodia—"

"Sure, sure, but what about Cathy? Is he going to
break up with her?"

"Oh, we never talk about that. . . . Sometime he talk
about football. He such a big star, but I don't think he so
happy about it."

"Really? That's weird."

Sundara closed her locker and leaned back on it.
"Kelly? Will your parents let you go on a date?"

"*Let* me? Are you kidding? My mother would *die* for
me to have a date. She's always bugging me about boys,
and believe me, I don't appreciate being reminded I don't
have anything to hide."

Sundara sighed. "I have something to hide—and it
scare me to death!"

In spite of her fears, Sundara found herself letting Jonathan fall in step beside her every day after international
relations. Then she would follow him with her lunch tray
to their special place on the patio. She watched herself
doing this, day after day, almost as if she were watching
someone else. So daring! Yet somehow the risk made her
moments with Jonathan all the sweeter.

Then one day, when she had almost grown compla-
cent, her luck ran out.

"I never understand why the American student so

noisy in class," she was telling Jonathan as they finished
their lunches. "Don't they want a good education?"

"Sure, I guess, but—"

"In my country, you get goofy like that—whap, whap
—you gonna get it with a stick on your back!"

"They *beat* you?"

"Oh, yes. Or one teacher I have, he pinch your ear like
this." She demonstrated, pretending to yank her gold ear-
ring.

"Sounds pretty rough."

"Well, they don't have to do that too much, because
most of the student have good behavior. They know they
must learn; they gonna be in big trouble at home if their
parent find out they not respecting the teacher. But here
. . ." She shook her head. "Even you! I'm shock when
you get so sassy, ask so many question. Like yesterday in
international relations when everybody argue? That
make me kind of nervous."

"That was just a good discussion. Lanegren *wants* everyone to get involved."

"He like it when the student argue with him? In my
country, you don't even dare ask the teacher to repeat if
you don't understand. That like saying he doing a bad job
of explaining. Same thing if somebody your boss."

"But if everybody's always pretending they understand when they don't, doesn't that lead to lots of misun-
derstandings?"

She frowned. "Sometime. But we don't like to argue
about that face-to-face. We rather smooth it over, keep everything nice, try to understand without having a . . .
what you call it?"

"A confrontation?"

"Yes! That the word. I'm shock when the American argue so much. Why you do this?"

"Beats me. I didn't know we did. Maybe we're just used to saying what we think."

"But sometime that so rude!"

He laughed. "Hey, Sundara, guess what?"

"What?"

"You're arguing!"

"Oh, you! You always make fun of—"

She stopped dead. Across the patio—Pok Simo with his Chinese friend. She held her breath, willing herself invisible. He hadn't seen her yet. But then his friend spotted her. He nudged Pok Simo.

Pok Simo took in their little scene—the lunch trays on the bench, the notebooks unopened. His eyes narrowed to a hard glare. She turned away, trembling. What fate! Of all people to walk by and find her alone with a white skin. For Pok Simo would love nothing better than to get her in trouble.

"You know him?" Jonathan asked.

She nodded, feeling sick. "He is Khmer also." Pok Simo resented the fact that her uncle had risen to the position of accountant while his father, once a high military attaché, now worked as a janitor. He resented even more Sundara's proud way of walking through the halls, her refusal to give him the deferential nod due one of high rank. Sundara shivered. He would savor his revenge in spreading this story.

"Is he gone yet?"

"Yeah, he took off. But what's his problem?"

She shook her head distractedly. Better if she had humbly bowed to Pok Simo each time they'd passed in the school halls, declaring herself lower than the dust beneath his feet. Now, for holding her head high, she would pay. Because what would Soka do if word of a white skin reached her ears?

News traveled fast among the Cambodians; Sundara did not expect to be kept in suspense long.

The following morning, her aunt's voice, harsher than usual, rudely ended Sundara's dream, a dream that somehow combined the warmth of Jonathan's smile with the softness of a night in Phnom Penh. Which was worse, the shattering nightmares, or waking from such loveliness at the snap of Soka's voice? Cold fear rushed through her as she remembered the previous day. Was it possible her aunt had already heard Pok Simo's story?

Sundara took her quick turn in the bathroom, washing her face, touching on some makeup, staring at her reflection. Did she look like a wicked girl? A girl who ate lunch alone with a boy? She would miss talking with him. Never before had anyone seemed so interested in her life, her feelings. What a relief it had been to speak of things so long held inside.

When she came into breakfast wearing jeans and a jade green blouse, Soka gave her one of those accusing looks. "You spend a lot of time on yourself lately."

Sundara swallowed. She *had* taken extra care in winding the ends of her hair around the curling iron, but her clothes were nothing special, except in comparison to Soka's. Soka refused to buy clothes for herself, and wished Sundara would also refrain. But Sundara didn't want to dress out of charity boxes as she'd had to at first. What fate! All those horrible pants suits of stretchy material . . . They were nothing like what the other girls were wearing. Not that she ever missed looking *exactly* like everyone else as she had at home, skipping to school each day in a blue skirt and white blouse. It was just that now she wanted to fit in with the Americans. She wanted jeans and tops like everyone else.

"Little ones! Come eat!" Soka had set their places to eat around the table western style. Now she poured the sugary cereal the boys had seen advertised on television.

Pon punched off his cartoons and carried in the jar of strawflowers he'd been wiring for Mr. Bonner's wife. He earned two cents for each stem he attached.

"Wonderful!" Soka said. "At least three dollars' worth. What a clever son." She gave his cheek a quick nuzzle. "Ravy, here is your note for the school."

"What's this?" Naro wanted to know as Ravy stuffed the paper in the back pocket of his jeans and sat down.

"The school called," Soka said. "They wanted me to write my permission so he can play football after school."

"Football? Ravy, why do you want to smash into other people?"

"It's flag football, Papa, not tackle. You just yank the flag out of the other guy's pocket."

Sundara and Ravy exchanged glances. She knew very well he could hardly wait to play tackle.

"Talking to those people at his school is like pouring water on a duck's back," Soka complained. "No matter how many times I tell them, I cannot make them understand that I am not Mrs. Tep, there *is* no Mrs. Tep. I am Kem Soka, I tell them on the phone yesterday, but it does no good."

"You should give up trying to put *Kem* first," Naro said. "It only confuses them."

She took a seat. "Well, I can understand that. But why

is it so difficult for them to understand a married woman keeping the name she is born with? *They* invented this women's lib, not us."

"Haven't you learned yet?" Naro said. "This is their country. They don't care about our ways. We are expected to imitate *them.*"

"And some of their ways I don't mind. But I'll tell you one thing, these children of ours must not become too American." She took each of them in with her eyes. "We don't want those bad things happening to the children of *this* family. Drinking, drugs, getting pregnant . . ."

Sundara's face got hot. She couldn't help it—Soka's black eyes boring into her like that. If her aunt's vague suspicions were this hard to endure, imagine how terrifying to face her wrath at the truth!

Her cousins had gobbled their cereal and excused themselves. They went back down the hall to collect Ravy's homework papers and Pon's toy motorcycle for first grade show-and-tell.

"The best American idea, as far as I'm concerned," Soka went on, "is a man being allowed only one wife at a time." She gave Naro a pointed look, then turned back to Sundara. "At home, Niece, if you get a good husband who makes a lot of money, there will always be younger women coming around, wanting to be wife number two. A terrible nuisance."

Sundara kept her eyes on her noodles, unable to enjoy the rare hint of intimacy in Soka's voice. Even if this old quarrel had lost its heat for Soka and Naro, it still served as an ominous reminder of her aunt's temper. To this day Sundara recalled overhearing her own parents discussing it—something about a younger woman, and Soka taking an ax to Naro's prized motorcycle. Sundara shuddered. Soka was not a good person to cross.

And how treacherously close Sundara always felt to Soka's anger. It was do this, don't do that, every minute of the day. Now that Soka had her food-service job at the university, she seemed to have completely forgotten how much she had depended on Sundara that first year, how much Sundara had helped her, answering the phone, going to the door while Soka cowered in the bedroom as if expecting to be dragged away. . . . For a while Sundara had hoped all this might win Soka's forgiveness for the baby's death, but when Soka became strong again and unafraid, she also turned meaner than ever, as if blaming Sundara for her own period of helplessness.

Now her aunt spoke to Naro with excessive sweetness. "You're better off here, I think, where you can't talk to other women so much."

"You mean *you're* better off," he teased. "You know, you ought to watch how much *you* become American, Little Sister. You've put yourself high up enough in this family as it is."

"Too bad!" Soka replied, suppressing a smile, jutting her chin out at him.

"Oh Niece," Naro said with mock weariness, "why did my parents match me with such a sassy woman?"

Soka smiled broadly at this. She had good, even teeth, and a very nice look about her, Sundara thought, when she was joking with someone she liked. And they all knew Naro was only teasing, for Soka had proven a good wife to him. Especially after the first year in America, when he sank into depression. He, who had supported so many relatives at home, shamed by having to send his wife to work! But while he brooded in silence those long months, waiting for time to heal his spirit, Soka had been the most loyal and loving of wives.

Now he grinned at her. "At least she is better than the wife of Pok Sary." He jerked up his arms as if to ward off her blow.

"Ha! You *better* think so."

"I saw the two of them yesterday," he said. "Let me tell you, this is what *I* like about America: Here I don't have to bow down to *them*. You should have heard them, boasting about that son of theirs. It makes me tired."

Sundara's pulse raced at the mere mention of Pok Simo. Nervously she rose to fill her bowl again, hoping they wouldn't notice her hands shaking.

"You would think," Soka said, "that if they were so high-class they would have the good manners not to brag."

Naro nodded. "I've often thought that myself. I don't know how many times I've heard about their big brick house in Phnom Penh, their car, how everybody wanted to be their friend."

"I suppose we should try to be understanding," Soka said. "Perhaps we would feel the same way if we fell so low from so high up. But still . . ."

"Where's Grandmother?" Sundara said. "Not well again?"

Soka turned in her chair and gave Sundara one of those measuring looks. Had her attempt to change the subject been too obvious?

But to Sundara's relief, Soka merely sighed. "She doesn't want to eat. She doesn't even want to get out of bed today. Sometimes it seems hopeless. I finally persuade her to come to the supermarket with me, and then the checker is so rude Grandmother says she won't ever go back."

"They just don't have any respect for the elderly, do they?" Naro said. "And sometimes, Little Sister, I don't think *you* show her the respect she deserves, either."

"Me!" Soka was indignant. "What about you? You're not exactly humbling yourself for her advice all the time."

This stopped him. "Well, it's different here."

"Yes," she snapped, "I've noticed that." Then her voice softened. "I'm sorry, Naro. I do the best I can with your mother, but as you say, it's different here, and what can she tell us about coping with life in America when all she does is stay in the house, dreaming of home?"

"Ah, so understanding America is the way to be respected, then? If that's so, perhaps we should all fall on our knees before young Ravy!"

"Ha! Or Sundara here."

Oh, no. How American Sundara Has Become. A topic Soka relished and Sundara loathed. So unfair, to be criticized for everything right down to what Soka claimed was her overly bold way of walking. If only her aunt could see what an outsider she was at school. What did Soka think? That she could go to an American school and squat in the cafeteria to eat as if she were still half a world away? Would that have satisfied her? At home Sundara was too American; at school she felt painfully aware of not being American enough. She didn't fit in anywhere. *Please don't start on this,* she thought.

Fortunately, Soka seemed more inclined, at the moment, to analyze Grandmother's problems. "She has nothing like school or a job to force her out of the house. If only we could find something . . ." She considered this for a moment, then jumped up. "As for me, I have more than enough to do. That's the answer, you see. Work. Keep busy. Then there's less time to brood. Niece, you will start the dinner tonight so we can eat as soon as I get home. I promised to take that new family shopping for warm clothes tonight."

"They're having a sale at Valu-Time," Sundara offered, trying to be helpful. Unable to bargain here, Soka liked to at least find the best sales.

But Soka waved away that suggestion. "Last time I bought a jacket there the threads unraveled after one washing. I thought everything here would be good quality, but you really have to be careful."

Sundara nodded. The jacket she'd put on layaway for herself was at one of the nice stores downtown. But Soka would consider that an extravagance, and would like it even less if she knew Sundara hadn't waited to walk in with cash. But after one more payday she'd have enough, and what if the beautiful plum-colored jacket were gone by then?

She scooped out the last of the noodles from the pot into her bowl, causing her aunt to cluck.

"That's your third bowl! I don't know why you're not fat, all the food you eat and nothing but sitting in school all day."

"I'm sorry," Sundara said meekly. "I should have asked if either of you would like the rest. Would you?"

Naro shook his head and Soka said she'd had enough— she was getting a bit plump herself lately—so Sundara ate the noodles. But Soka had spoiled her appetite.

Once out the door, Sundara began to breathe easier. Nothing said about Pok Simo. She sank into her bus seat thinking maybe she'd be lucky this time. Maybe they wouldn't find out. If she stayed away from Jonathan from now on, there was still a chance she might save herself.

And after all, was he really worth the risk? Maybe

Cathy was right. Maybe she *was* just a curiosity to him. Maybe she was making a fool of herself, letting herself care about him as if there were the slightest chance they could ever belong to the same world.

Besides, she already had one failure on her conscience: the death of Soka's baby. There was no more room in her life for mistakes, large or small.

Yes, what she must do was quite clear. She would not think of him. She would not waste any more time looking for him in the halls. She would study hard during lunch hour the way she used to, and when her parents came they would be proud. She would not talk to him. She would not look at him. She would forget it ever happened.

And then the school bus pulled up to the patio. Through the tinted window, she saw him standing by the flagpole. What was he doing there all by himself? Usually she didn't see him until international relations. He looked so nice. She loved those faded jeans and that flannel shirt of his. The morning sun shone on his blond hair as he tapped his notebook against his thigh and looked around.

Her heart pounded, her knees felt weak as she stood up in the bus aisle. She must pretend she hadn't seen him and walk past to the building. With so many students milling around, maybe she'd escape his notice.

But when she stepped off the bus, he hurried right toward her. He had been waiting especially for her. He knew which bus she rode.

"Sundara! I've got to talk to you." He led her away from the others. His hand on her arm felt nice, nicer than it should have. "How about explaining that little scene yesterday. Is that guy your boyfriend or something?"

She glanced up at him in surprise. "Oh, no! He be mad to hear you say this. We not the same class."

"So? Lots of girls go out with older guys. I thought—"

"Not class in school! *Social class,* don't you know? Oh, too hard to explain now." She looked over her shoulder. Were they being watched?

"But why'd you run off, then?"

"Because he *see* us. With my people everyone watch everyone else. He will talk."

"We were just sitting there."

"But I am a girl and you are a boy!"

"You noticed that too, huh?"

"Oh, you make fun!" Her voice wavered between a giggle and a wail; her cheeks were warm. "I could get in trouble. How many times do I have to tell you? In Cambodia a girl doesn't go with a boy alone."

"You're in America now."

"Oh, is that so?" She made a face. "Sometime I forget!"

He grinned. "Meet me for lunch?"

"Jonatan." So persistent! Was it possible he really didn't understand? How blunt you sometimes had to be with Americans! But the longer she stayed there with him in the fresh morning air, the easier it was to let herself be persuaded, the harder it was to tell him they must not see each other. Soka had a strong power over her, but so did Jonathan.

And right now, as he stood looking at her with those strange and lovely blue eyes, she just *liked* him, liked the way he made her feel, liked the way he was banishing her nightmares by stealing into her dreams. Was that so terrible? After all, it was not as if staying away from him would bring the baby back to life. . . .

"Okay," she said. "I meet you." And her heart beat with the most extraordinary mixture of joy and fear.

CHAPTER 8

Sundara was used to being watched.

In Willamette Grove, black hair and brown skin stood out. Except for a few people up at the university, almost everyone was white. So when she'd first come here, people stared because she was different.

Then, more recently, she'd noticed the boys paying a new kind of attention, boldly eyeing her from head to foot, hanging on their lockers or elbowing each other as she passed.

And of course there was always Soka, monitoring her for the slightest sign of disobedience. After four years, Sundara had almost forgotten what life was like without those watchful eyes, the automatic looks of disapproval at her every move.

But now she had Jonathan. How much nicer it was to have *him* studying her. In his eyes she read only good messages: *You are beautiful. You are special. I could look at you all day long.* The intensity of his gaze across the classroom was difficult to ignore. She could almost feel the heat of it. And other people were starting to notice too.

Kelly assured her that everyone was talking. Now even the girls were looking at her. Conversations seemed to trail off when she walked by. Heads turned.

"What do you expect?" Kelly said. "Everybody can see he's absolutely smitten with you."

"Smitten?"

"Knocked out, crazy over, totally infatuated. Like that. People can't help being curious. They're all wondering like, *who* is this exotic creature they've heard about."

Apparently the stir was not lost on Jonathan's coach, either. One day on the patio Sundara looked up to see him watching them from the door of the faculty lunchroom.

"Is that your coach?" she asked Jonathan.

He took a quick look. "Yeah."

"What the matter? Why does he watch us?"

"Just likes to keep an eye on all the players." He turned back and gave the coach a lazy salute.

Hackenbruck nodded, not smiling.

"He look kind of mean," Sundara whispered.

"Huh. That's probably one of the nicer words people use."

Finally, Hackenbruck went back inside.

"Why he so mad?"

"Oh, he has this thing about girls. Thinks you sap our energy. Get us all distracted."

"Oh." She was thinking of Cathy. Did the coach watch Jonathan when he was with her? "He mad about you eat lunch with me?"

Jonathan shrugged. "It's a bunch of stuff. He called me in the other day. Give me a lot of crap about buckling down, getting my head in the right space. I guess he's got a right to that, but when he starts getting into my personal life . . . Well, I just told him I thought what I did off the field was my own business. But he says anything that affects my performance *is* his business. Says I'm getting a bad attitude about football." He shrugged again. "Guess I really can't argue with that."

"You don't like football anymore? Even though you the star?"

"Hey, I signed up to play a game, not fight a war. You should hear Hackenbruck in the locker room. Smash 'em, pound 'em, kill 'em . . ." He tossed the last of his taco back on the tray. "Other things bug me too. Like the game last week. Did you see that guy get his knee torn up? Everybody goes, 'Hey, we gotta win for Baker.' But I kept thinking, wait a minute, winning's not going to fix his knee."

Sundara waited to make sure he was finished. "Why do you play, then? Why you don't quit?"

"I don't know. It's hard to explain. Being on the team gets so tied in to who you are."

She nodded. "Make you important. I see how everybody kind of bow down to the player."

"Well, not everybody. Plenty of people don't give a hoot about football." He jerked his head toward a group huddled at the curb, smoke rising from whatever they were passing around. "Like those guys. They couldn't care less." He turned back to her. "And the brains. You

won't catch them at a pep rally when they could be log-
ging time in the computer room."

He was right, Sundara realized. She'd been so busy
trying to understand exactly what Americans were like,
she'd missed the point. Americans were all sorts of things.

"Anyway," he went on, "I don't need people putting
me on a pedestal. It's more just this pressure of having to
be what everybody wants me to be. My parents and all."

She nodded. "Your family honor."

He laughed. "If you want to put it that way."

"They probably so proud when you win the game."

"I guess. But it's weird. I don't think they were into
sports when they were younger. They were busy marching for civil rights and all that. Sometimes they kid around
like, 'How on earth did we get a football player for a son?'
But they come to all the games. I hear my mom on the
phone bragging about me. So I guess it's pretty important
to them. But sometimes I wish I had the nerve to say,
'Hey, does being able to run fast and catch a ball mean I
have to do it?' "

She thought for a moment. "Jonatan?"

"Hmm?"

"You the same person to me if you play football or
not."

For a moment he just looked at her, then his hand
came toward her cheek.

She flinched.

"Sorry." He pulled back. "I forget."

For a long time neither said anything. Finally, Jonathan spoke.

"You know, it's funny. My friend Clarkston, he has
this theory that I'm going to have a terrible crisis someday

when I don't get something I really want. Says everything's always come too easily for me."

"You cannot help that you smart and can run fast."

He rested his forearms on his thighs and stared at the ground. "But maybe he's right. I'm beginning to see that now. Before, I didn't know what it was to really *long* for something." He turned and gave her a crooked smile. "Now I do."

Cathy Gates pushed through the swinging door into the lavatory, flanked by two friends. Spotting Sundara, she switched on her smile.

"Oh, hi, Sundara!"

Sundara's brush stopped in midair. "Hi."

Cathy eased into the spot next to her at the mirror and took out a tube of lip gloss. "I love your hair," she told Sundara's reflection.

Sundara saw her own mouth twitch in a nervous smile as she started brushing again. She glanced at the girl next to her, Jan Cheney. They'd been talking about their latest assignment for English comp when Cathy interrupted. Now Jan went on about how she never knew what to write, but Sundara was too nervous really to follow her.

Cathy took out a brush and fluffed her hair around her face. Toilets flushed. The warning bell sounded.

"See you later," Jan, said, heading into the hall with the rest of the girls.

Sundara remained beside Cathy, slowly pulling the brush through her already thoroughly brushed hair. Such a terrible silence. But what did you say to the girlfriend of a boy you liked? I love your hair too?

Finally, Cathy dropped her brush into her bag and

turned to face Sundara. "Don't you think we ought to talk about this?" Her voice echoed in the tiled room.

Sundara smiled with embarrassment. "I don't know what you want me to say."

Cathy laughed. "I'm not trying to make you say anything in particular. I just want to know what you're thinking."

Sundara hesitated. She was thinking she'd never been this close to Cathy before. Her perfume smelled like some kind of fruit. And under her makeup, all across her nose and cheeks, she had lots of those little flyspecks—freckles, the Americans called them. She was sure Cathy didn't want to hear about that, though.

"I'm thinking you're mad with me," she said.

"Oh, come on." Cathy tossed an amused smile back at her friends. "Why would I be mad?"

Sundara kept her eyelids lowered. "Maybe because Jonatan like me?"

Cathy blinked, then regained her composure. "Oh, Sundara, of course Jonathan likes you. I like you too. Everybody does."

Sundara understood the phony smile. Cathy wanted her to think that Jonathan only liked her in the same friendly way everyone else did.

"That's why I honestly don't want to see you get hurt. Believe me, I've been through this before. You're not the first girl who's gone after him."

Sundara drew a swift breath. "I never go after him."

"Well, you know what I mean."

"No, I don't. Jonatan ask me about my story for his report and I say okay. Does that mean I go after him?"

Cathy exchanged glances with her red-haired friend, the one so thin, she seemed to be starving, then turned back to Sundara and let out a long, disgusted sigh. "Okay, I've tried to be nice about it, but look—Jonathan and I have been going together since the ninth grade. We have something *very special* between us."

Sundara gripped her brush. Were they sleeping together? She thought of the first time she'd seen them walking down the hall, hands in the back pockets of each other's jeans . . .

"Very special," Cathy repeated. "So don't try to mess it up." She whirled on her heel and strode out the door. Her friends followed, glancing back to check Sundara's reaction.

She was shaking. Americans! They didn't avoid confrontations; they *enjoyed* them! And Cathy certainly had the advantage in this one. Sundara suspected she had even practiced what to say beforehand.

Only later did Sundara think of a good reply. She imagined herself holding up her head, looking Cathy straight in the eye. "It's a free country," she should have said. "And I can like any boy I want!"

But then, it wouldn't have been true.

Not for her.

CHAPTER 9

Sundara marveled as she parked the station wagon in front of Jonathan's huge white house. So big for only three people! Why did the Americans want all this space around them? Didn't they like to be close with their families? The yard was impressive, too, with these venerable old trees. She couldn't help comparing them to the pathetic twigs in her own yard. The McKinnons' home had a look of permanence, as if the people inside had never lived anywhere else but right here.

Stomach fluttering, she climbed the sun-dappled brick steps. Was she really going to do this? Had she, Sundara Sovann, really accepted an invitation to go sailing with an American family? Without telling Soka?

It had seemed like fate—Jonathan asking her to come on the very weekend her aunt and uncle were going to Portland without her, leaving her behind to work the final Saturday market. And it wasn't a real date, Jonathan assured her. So how could she resist?

Resisting Jonathan was, after all, very difficult. At home each evening under Soka's watchful eyes, Sundara promised herself she would stop seeing him. But each morning at school, she quickly forgot her resolve. What harm in one more lunch together? And one more and one more . . . And now here she was.

Drawing herself up, she flipped back her braid and aimed a trembling finger at the doorbell, touching off a lovely peal of chimes.

In a moment the massive green door opened and there was Jonathan, looking a little shy himself.

"Hi. Come on in." He called into another room, "She's here, Mom."

Mrs. McKinnon appeared in the dining room arch. "Sundara," she said. "Finally! I've been so anxious to meet you."

Sundara could only smile, wavering between a formal Khmer bow and some proper American response she couldn't quite formulate. Mrs. McKinnon surprised her. She'd been expecting fancier clothes, more makeup, an American mother like on TV. Instead, in plain old jeans and a sweater, here stood this blond woman with the most open, fresh-scrubbed face.

"Jonathan's told us a lot about you."

"Oh . . ." Sundara looked to Jonathan.

"All good stuff," he put in, grinning.

Mrs. McKinnon kept smiling at her, taking her in with frank curiosity. Usually this American way of staring was

unnerving, but Sundara sensed an innocence in Mrs. Mc-
Kinnon's expression. She wasn't trying to judge or pry.
Her look was somehow flattering. *I'm interested in you,* she
seemed to be saying.

Sundara found herself smiling back into her blue eyes,
the blue eyes she'd passed on to Jonathan.

"Is Dad ready?" Jonathan asked.

"He should be." His mother gripped the polished
newel post and shouted up the stairs. "Ri-chard? Sundara's
here!"

From the upper reaches of the house a man's voice
rumbled. "Where did you hide my Top-Siders?"

"Right on your shoe rack," she called back.

"I want my *old* ones!"

"There," Mrs. McKinnon said to Sundara with a wry
smile. "Now you can see why Jonathan dresses the way he
does!" She headed up the stairs.

Mrs. McKinnon wasn't dressed so fancy herself, Sundara thought. Still, although her sweater was not new, it
was of good quality and color—a subtle shade of dusty
rose you'd never see at Valu-Time.

That was the look of their whole house, Sundara decided. Fine quality worn to a comfortable familiarity. She
had been in so few American homes—their sponsor's, and
Kelly's, and the home of the people from the church
who'd hosted their welcoming party. Those houses were
nice, but they could not compare to this.

Off to the left of the entryway she could see the living
room with its velvety, russet-toned furniture. And their
plush carpeting—no plastic runners! You were free to
walk right on it, let your tennis shoes sink deep into its
softness. To the right, in the dining room, she was drawn
toward a chandelier hung with bits of flashing glass that

caught and scattered the morning sunlight into rainbows on the pale gold wallpaper.

It's almost a palace, she thought. Yet Mrs. McKinnon did not act like a queen. And there were newspapers on the sofas, magazines and bills on the dining table. They treated it as if it were nothing special.

"Your family must live here for many generations," Sundara whispered.

Jonathan laughed. "Not quite. We moved here when I was six. Before that we were up in Seattle while my dad did his residency."

"Oh." Hard to believe. It all looked so . . . established. "Your mother have to work hard to clean such a big house. She have so many pretty thing to dust off."

"Well, we have a housekeeper who comes in."

"You joking. A servant?"

"No, not a servant. Just somebody to vacuum and stuff. Of course, she can't do my room. It's too much of a mess."

"But Jonatan, I'm shock!"

"Why? It's no big deal."

"Oooh . . . but when we mention to our sponsor that we have servant in Cambodia she get kind of mad at us. 'Just forget that,' she say. 'We don't have servant in America. People gonna frown about that!' We so scared! Soka tell me never talk about that again."

"Hmm. That's interesting. You didn't have a telephone or television, but you had servants."

"Someone to help with the dishes is better than a television, I think. Then you have more time to play with the children or have a lot of friend over, listen to music. We never have enough time here. Just work, work, work."

"That's why it's so good you decided to come today.

You gotta have *some* fun. You work too hard. You're always lugging around that huge stack of books."

"Now I never read, though!" She laughed. "That *your* fault. Before, I study all the time at lunch. Now I probably flunk *every*thing." She picked up a newspaper clipping from a pile on the dining table. "Oh, picture of you!"

"Yeah. Didn't you see that in the paper?"

She shook her head. Naro and Soka didn't take the paper. "But what is this?" She looked more closely at the large book that lay open beside the clippings. "Everything is about you?"

" 'Fraid so. It's a scrapbook. You know, for pasting things you want to save. My mom's been working on it since I was born. Didn't you do that in Cambodia?"

Sundara could only smile. The things worth saving could not be pasted in a book. Glue and paper could not preserve the comfort of familiar voices, the good smell of her mother cooking chicken with garlic and lemon grass over the charcoal stove . . .

She flipped through the pages. So many football pictures. "You famous!" she said. "The book is so fat!"

"And this is the third volume. I wish my mom wouldn't get so carried away."

"Why not? I think she like you a lot, want to spoil you."

"Yeah, I guess, but sometimes I feel like she thinks my main job in life is to come up with stuff for these books."

Perhaps it was because she had only one child, Sundara thought. Only one son on whom to lavish all her love.

"Does your mother have a job? My aunt say all American women have job."

"Well, not really. But she's president of the League of Women Voters around here, so that takes a lot of time."

"What is that? League of Women Voters?"

"Oh, they study politics, social problems and stuff."

"Sound important."

"I guess."

Sundara was thinking about Soka. Maybe she only told Naro all women worked outside their homes so he would stop feeling so guilty about her having to do it.

"Here's the scrapbook I'm keeping for international relations." He tapped a thinner book. "Clippings about Cambodia."

Sundara flipped open the book and read one headline: CAMBODIANS STARVE BY THE THOUSANDS. She shut it.

Jonathan's father came down the wide stairs, his size surprising Sundara all over again. He had sprouted a few gray hairs in his neatly trimmed beard, yet in his casual clothes he seemed younger than he had four years ago, when she'd seen him only in his stiff white coat. He smiled. His brown eyes had lost none of their warmth.

"How are you, Sundara? How's that little cousin of yours?"

"Oh, he very well, thank you." He remembered! "Hard to believe he ever so skinny."

"Are we all ready, then?" Mrs. McKinnon asked, coming down after him. "Let's load up."

At that moment Sundara caught a glimpse of herself in the mirror over the sideboard. She froze, startled by her own reflection. But why? Had she forgotten for a moment that her hair was black, her skin darker than theirs? How strangely out of place she looked.

Outside, they got into a jeep-type truck with an empty boat trailer behind it.

Sundara whispered to Jonathan, "My cousin Ravy really like this kind of car. He want to get one someday."

"Yeah, the four-wheel drive is great, especially for going to the mountains. Maybe we could go skiing sometime. Want to?"

She nodded, overwhelmed. She could hardly believe she was actually going on this one trip with him today and he was already making *more* plans.

The rush of air by the open windows made conversation difficult, but it didn't matter. Sundara was caught up in her thoughts, anyway. What a risk she'd taken. . . . What if— Oh, forget Soka! If her aunt never learned of the lunches at school, how could she possibly hear about this? Besides, the decision was made now, and whatever the consequences, she was here, sitting beside Jonathan with the sun shining and the smell of autumn in the air. Why not enjoy it?

"Can you believe our luck?" Dr. McKinnon said when they pulled into the parking lot at the lake an hour later. "Practically got the whole place to ourselves." The concession stand was boarded up. Only a few boats dotted the water. The sweeping lawns were all but deserted.

"Gorgeous weather for October," Mrs. McKinnon said. "Sure does make it hard to pull the boat out."

"Why must you?" Sundara followed them out onto the long wooden dock. "Does everyone have to?" She had noticed another boat being hooked up to a trailer at the launch, and many of the mooring places were empty.

"They've already started to let the water out," Dr. McKinnon explained. "It's a man-made reservoir—irrigation in the summer, flood control in the winter."

So much of America was man-made, Sundara thought, looking out over the smooth water. Imagine. Men even controlled the lakes and rivers. How different from the mighty Mekong, never bridged nor dammed, which rose so high in the rainy season, flooding the rice paddies with the melted snow of the far-off Himalayas, turning the Tonle Sap into an inland sea. That great lake drained itself in its *own* time.

"Welcome aboard the *Bonnie Lass,* Sundara." Dr. McKinnon helped her step down into the boat and Jonathan guided her to the bench seat. They sat facing his parents.

"I'm afraid this won't be the most thrilling sail we've ever had," Mrs. McKinnon said. "Not much wind."

Thrilling enough, Sundara thought as Jonathan's shoulder came to rest against hers. The sails caught the slight breeze, easing the boat away from the dock.

Now they were under way. Without the business of loading and setting off to occupy them, the silence began to seem awkward.

"Well," Mrs. McKinnon said, "it's really nice that you could come, Sundara."

Sundara smiled. Once more she wished she could simply offer a Khmer-style bow. A respectful nod of the head. But Americans expected you to talk.

Jonathan's parents traded a quick question with their eyes. Maybe they didn't know what to say either.

Dr. McKinnon cleared his throat. "Jonathan's told us about how you got to America, having to spend all that time on the boat." Another glance at his wife, a hesitation. Then he tried again. "The thing is, when you and your family came into the clinic that first time . . . I'm afraid I just didn't . . . *realize* . . ."

"Oh, I shouldn't complain about that," Sundara said, rescuing him. "Many people have a much harder time. Some have to stay in a refugee camp for many month, even a year or two. And all the boat people coming now—compare to them, we so lucky."

She paused. Dr. McKinnon seemed relieved to have her do the talking. They all seemed to be waiting for more.

"Like the story about the lady who cry to Buddha because of her bad luck. You know this one? He tell her that her trouble will go away if she bring a seed from a house that has never known sorrow. The next week he find her singing so happy. When the Enlightened One ask if she find the Seed of Happiness, she say, 'No, Enlightened One. At every house I find trouble worse than my own. So I now believe I am truly quite fortunate.' "

They were all smiling at her. Obviously, they liked the story. And it did contain much wisdom. Look at the McKinnons. With all their blessings, even their house could not produce the Seed of Happiness. Not when their hopes for more children had been dashed so many times.

While they ate their sandwiches, Jonathan's parents started telling about different sails they'd taken, and teased each other with stories, like the time Dr. McKinnon jumped out to pull the boat to shore and went in over his head. He insisted on describing all the features of his boat, which meant nothing to Sundara, of course, no more than the boat's odd name: *Bonnie Lass.*

Then Mrs. McKinnon gathered up the paper plates. "Jonathan tells us you want to be a doctor," she said.

Sundara nodded, glancing at Jonathan, wondering if he'd also told them how much she admired his father. "My family want me to become a doctor so maybe someday I can go back to Cambodia with World Vision or the Red Cross."

Children of the River

Dr. McKinnon's bushy eyebrows went up. "That's quite a goal."

He seemed surprised. Maybe he didn't think she was smart enough. She still did not meet his eyes, but lifted her chin a little. "I am hoping to go to Stanford."

"Good choice!"

They were all smiling at her again.

"We went there," Mrs. McKinnon explained. "That's where we met."

Sundara smiled back, grateful she had managed to say the right thing. So difficult sometimes! She liked the American ideal of everyone being equal—even a peanut farmer could be President—but at times like this she missed the strict rules one followed in Kampuchea. At home she would have known their respective ranks and spoken accordingly, but here it was all so treacherously free and loose. A person might make a terrible mistake without even knowing it. Show too much respect and they thought you cringing; not enough, and you were rebellious. For there *were* different ranks of people. She knew now that even the Americans divided their people into classes—they just didn't like to admit it by spelling out the rules.

"So your aunt and uncle are planning to put you through college?"

"Dad, what is this, the Inquisition?"

But Sundara smiled. "My aunt say—" She stopped. Too personal to mention, how her aunt hated to spend money on a girl's education when there was always the risk—however slight—that she might get pregnant. "My aunt want me to try for a scholarship."

"Ah. Well, Stanford does have a good financial-aid program. Grades pretty good, are they? When you apply, maybe I could help with a recommendation."

"Oh, thank you." He spoke as if college and medical school were a real possibility for her. Something that might actually happen. But perhaps this was merely the way of people used to making plans and counting on the future.

"Let's sit up front," Jonathan said.

Balancing carefully as she followed him to the bow, she braced herself on the top of the cabin. Glancing back at Dr. McKinnon, she was startled when he winked at her. *Winked.*

"Glad to have you on board, Sundara."

It was another world, sitting with Jonathan, their bare toes on the sun-warmed fiber glass deck. She liked the way the sun lit the gold hairs on his arms and the breeze tousled his hair. Who could have imagined she'd ever find herself *enjoying* sitting on an open boat deck in the sun? But here she was, lifting her face to the warm rays without caring, the way the Americans did.

"Sorry about all the questions," Jonathan said. "I wish they wouldn't be that way."

"But I think they are so nice." It had not occurred to her he might be wondering what *she* thought of *them.*

She stole a peek back over her shoulder. Dr. McKinnon had one hand on that steering stick—she'd already forgotten what he called it—and the other arm around his wife. They looked happy together.

"Your parents—they choose each other to marry?"

Jonathan laughed. "Of course! Well, actually, sometimes Mom says it was all his idea and he says it was all her idea, but basically, yeah, they chose each other." He shook his head. "I should show you their wedding pictures. I can't believe they ever looked so young. My mom was going to be a social worker. Dad was going to do medical care for poor kids. They tell me that back then they were planning to change the world."

Change the world. What a funny idea. Only two westerners would dream of throwing themselves against the prearranged cosmic order of things. . . . Yet somehow, imagining the McKinnons in their idealistic younger days, she felt nothing but affection. After all, Dr. McKinnon *had* made a little part of her world better.

"So does your mother become a social worker?"

"Yeah, for a while. But then she had me and I guess she kind of burned out on all the sad cases."

"And your father?"

"He did quite a bit of volunteer work at this free clinic. Worked some with the Indians. But that was before we came here." He shrugged. "I guess they've pretty much given up on all that now."

She watched the sun flashing on the water as the boat bobbed up and down. "Something I wonder about—they don't mind I'm not white?"

"Sundara! What a crazy idea! I mean, they *better* not. All my life they've been telling me everybody's equal, race doesn't matter."

"Doesn't matter at all to them?"

"Well, theoretically."

Theoretically. They both knew saying you believed something was not the same as living it.

"But my dad's younger brother joined the Peace Corps and ended up marrying an Indonesian woman. Nobody was unhappy about *that*." He smiled at Sundara in a way that made her face warm. "Their kids are really cute."

Sundara looked into his eyes, blue with black ringing

the irises. If she had his baby, what color would the eyes be? Then they both blushed. Had he been wondering the same thing?

"I don't think my family ever going to feel that way," she said. "They don't even try to pretend race doesn't matter. And they don't like the American way about marriage and everything. Don't like so quick to divorce. Don't like to have the baby without the husband."

"Well, that isn't exactly our ideal either."

"But it happen all the time. This never happen with Khmer girl."

"Never?"

"Not if they are daughters of good family."

"But *never*? That's hard to believe."

"I do know one," she admitted. "A girl in Portland, she love a boy at a Thailand camp? They planning to marry but he go to France and her family come here. So her parents won't let her marry. They afraid they never see her again if she go to France." Sundara lowered her voice. "When they come here they find she going to have a baby."

"But they wanted to get married?"

"Oh, yes! She cry all the time for him. Keep saying he promise to find her and their baby someday."

"Why didn't he just come to America?"

"Cannot do that. So difficult to get a new country to accept, the people just have to go where they can."

They fell silent then as the boat made its lazy, gently rocking way across the water. How pleasant, Sundara thought, to let their shoulders touch this way, as if by accident, but neither of them moving away. If only she did not have to worry about Soka, about being a good Khmer girl. If only . . .

After a long time Jonathan finally spoke. "A penny for your thoughts."

Sundara started. "A penny for a thought? What does that mean?"

"Haven't you heard that expression? It means you have to tell me what you're thinking right at this instant."

Her eyes widened. "I have to tell my private thought? This is the American custom?"

He laughed. "I guess you don't really *have* to." He was studying her face. "But now I'm really curious. What *were* you thinking?"

"Oh . . ." She smiled, her cheeks warm with more than the sun. "I'm just thinking how I like this. How I wish it could always be this way."

"Well, why can't it?"

"Oh, Jonatan. You *know* why." She had tried so many times. But she couldn't explain something to him that he didn't want to understand.

He looked at her for a moment. "Sundara, do you— well, ever since I first saw you, I've had the strangest feeling. The way I was just drawn to you, like somehow I'd known you before . . ."

She spoke matter-of-factly. "You mean in our past lives?"

He blinked. "Well, I wasn't thinking of it so literally, but . . . this *feeling* . . ."

Sundara remembered that first time at the market, when she'd thought Jonathan reminded her of Chamroeun. Had it really been Chamroeun, or was the familiarity something else, something like recognizing a place you'd never been before, or meeting someone you'd been waiting for all your life?

"Yes," she said shyly, "I think I feel that way too."

They looked at each other for a moment, then he said, "You are just so unlike any girl I've ever known."

"That for sure." She flashed her dimples at him. "Black hair, black eye."

"I *love* your black hair, and your eyes aren't black, they're kind of a warm, melty brown."

"Oh, my skin too dark for you."

"Don't be stupid. You want to know the truth? I've got so used to looking at you, everybody else seems kind of washed-out in comparison."

"Is that true?"

He nodded. "And you know, as long as I'm confessing —at first when I started asking you to tell me about Cambodia?" He made a face. "I really just wanted an excuse to sit there and look at you. . . ."

She smiled. "I know."

"You know? You've known that all along?"

"Well, no, but after a while, like you say, I get the picture."

He grinned. "You're not mad?"

"No."

"Because I really did get interested in your stories. I wasn't faking that. They got to me. You started making me see how sheltered I was. That I'm actually pretty spoiled."

"Jonatan. You cannot help you have a nice life. Why you always feel so bad about it? Your family have the kind of life I want for myself. When I see how people can live here, I want to make that my goal."

"But you were just saying you wanted to be a doctor and help people."

"I do, but I also want a family and a house. I want to have enough money so I don't have to worry how am I gonna feed my children. I want to have a car so I can bring them to the pretty place like this. I want—"

"Coming about!" his father called, and suddenly the boat swung around and tipped, sails snapping. Sundara lurched toward the water, but just as fast, Jonathan's strong arm pulled her back. Her heart pounded and breath came hard. Was it the scare? Or the realization that he wasn't taking his arm away? . . . He was holding her tighter. Perhaps it was wrong, but she didn't care. At this moment, no power on earth could make her pull away from him.

And that's when he did it, a most surprising thing.

He reached across her with his free hand and gently tugged loose the crimson ribbon that held the end of her braid.

Startled, then understanding, she slowly undid the plait and combed her fingers through her hair, never taking her eyes from his. The breeze lifted the long black strands.

"It looks so pretty all loose like that."

A sudden puff of wind skittered the ribbon across the turquoise deck. "Whoops." Jonathan lunged, but the bit of velvet slipped through his fingers and blew overboard. "Sorry."

"That okay," she whispered, a restraining hand on his arm. She wouldn't need it. He liked her hair loose; she did not plan to braid it again.

CHAPTER 10

The next Saturday morning Naro, Soka, and Grandmother left Sundara in charge of the boys and started off
for the Chinese grocery store in Salem.

After she'd fastened the chain behind them, Sundara
leaned back against the door and sighed. She was not eager
to begin shucking the huge pile of corn they had just
gleaned from Mr. Bonner's fields. She hadn't minded gathering it. At least she'd been outside in the sparkling autumn morning. But now, to be stuck inside, knowing it
was another golden day out there . . . a golden day like
last Saturday, when she'd gone sailing with Jonathan.

Finally she went into the kitchen and dropped to a
crouch beside the corn, which was spread on a mat. But

before she could even make a start, the doorbell rang. She rose again, brushing off her sarong, and padded over to open the door. She peered out.

"Jonatan!" Hastily she unfastened the door chain.

"Hi. Hey, what's with the chain? This is Willamette Grove, remember?"

"Jonatan, why you come here?"

"I just thought I'd stop by and see if you wanted to go for a drive." Behind him she saw a tan sports car. He looked puzzled. "What's wrong?"

"My aunt and uncle go out. I supposed to take care my cousins." Lucky for her they *were* out. If Soka found a white skin on the front step asking for her . . .

"Oh. Well, when do you think they'll get back?"

"Jonatan." She shook her head, shuddering. He just didn't understand at all.

"Hey, this must be Pon."

Curious, the boys had left their TV football game and crept up behind her. Pon braved a look.

"Hi, buddy!" To Sundara's horror, Jonathan reached out and ruffled the little boy's hair.

Naturally, Pon pulled back, clinging to Sundara's sarong.

"You're not really supposed to do that," Ravy said.

"Ravy!"

"Well, we ought to tell him, don't you think?"

"What'd I do?" Jonathan said, bewildered.

"Cambodians think it's bad to touch a little kid's head," Ravy said. "It might make them lose their intelligence. Or their soul."

"Whoa! I wouldn't want to be responsible for that."

"Never mind," she said, a bit annoyed. Was he fighting a smile?

"I guess I should have called first," he said.

She shook her head. What good would that have done? It wasn't a question of calling ahead—her people didn't believe in that anyway. The problem was his being here at all. Look at him, standing there. Clearly he had no idea why he wasn't being treated to a warmer reception. But why hadn't he taken her seriously when she explained how her aunt and uncle felt about these things?

"I wish I can go," she said. "I really do." Her eyes flickered to the street behind him. It was probably safe to ask him in; wouldn't Soka herself say it was only proper to show respect to a guest, even an unexpected one? She hesitated. "Do you want to come in?"

He pointed to the the pairs of shoes lined up by the mat. "Am I supposed to take my shoes off?"

"You don't have to." She lowered her voice to a whisper and smiled. "It *is* good to see you."

She led the way into the living room, suddenly aware of the garlic smell that still lingered from last night's dinner. Would that bother him? What would he think of the plastic runners Soka insisted they walk on to protect the carpet? Perhaps their house was all wrong in ways she wasn't even aware of.

Seeing him looking at a collection of framed pictures on a cloth-covered table, Sundara picked one up. "This my family. One picture—that's all I have. Not much compare to your scrapbook!"

They smiled at each other, some of the familiar warmth returning. Together they looked at the photo: a handsome young couple with their three children.

"This Samet, Mayoury, and me." She sighed. "Look at my happy little-girl face."

"You were cute." He looked at her. "Still are."

Her palms flew to her cheeks. He had such a way of pulling her away from the past, keeping her right here in the present.

He was still studying the picture. "Is that background supposed to be Angkor Wat?"

She beamed. "You know a lot about my country." Who would imagine an American would know about the ancient temples her people had built in the jungle long ago?

"My report, you know."

Ravy stared up at Jonathan. "You really Jonathan McKinnon, the football player?"

"'Fraid so." Jonathan shifted from one foot to the other, making a face. "Maybe after last night I shouldn't admit it." The team had lost to North Salem.

"But still, when you went out for that pass . . . that was great! Boy, if I'd known you were *the* Jonathan McKinnon when I sold you those golf balls. . . ."

"I could've gotten a better deal?"

Ravy grinned. "I'm willing to negotiate in the future."

Jonathan laughed. He took another look around the room, his gaze coming to rest on a framed print, a girl with blond braids and wooden shoes standing in front of a windmill.

"I hope you won't think this is rude," he said, "but is there some special reason you've got a picture of Holland on your wall?"

Sundara had to giggle. "The church people give to us. We just hang up, you know, so the wall won't be empty? We don't even know what it is."

"You think that's weird," Ravy said, "you should have seen this place at first. It was two years before I figured it out and broke the news to my mom that everything she'd put up was supposed to be a Christmas decoration!"

Suddenly, the roar of a car in the driveway.

"Oh, no," Sundara whispered. "Somebody come."

"It's Mama," Pon called from the front door.

"Great," Jonathan said. "Maybe you can take off after all."

Sundara stared at him. If only she could make him disappear. She heard Pon reporting loudly in Khmer that a white skin had touched his head.

Soka came in. She gave Jonathan a sharp glance, then spread on a smile.

"This my aunt Soka," Sundara whispered. "She forget her list." Then, with lowered lids, she spoke in rapid Khmer, desperately explaining about Jonathan's report on Cambodia.

"Happy to meet Sundara school friend."

Jonathan was still looking open, vulnerable. Didn't he understand about smiles that were only for politeness?

"My parents were also happy to meet Sundara last weekend."

Heaven protect her, no! As Soka cocked her head, puzzled, Sundara made big eyes of alarm at Jonathan.

Clearly bewildered, Jonathan plunged ahead. "When she went sailing with us?"

Soka's eyes narrowed. Sundara shot him one last look of undiluted terror before fixing her gaze on the floor.

"I just stopped to see if Sundara wanted to go for a drive."

Soka forced another smile. "You too kind to my niece. We appreciate, but you too busy, have too many important thing to do."

"No, no, I'm not too busy. I'd really like to take her."

So *foolish*. Couldn't he see he was just making this

worse? Sundara clasped her hands, ready to beg for the mercy she was going to need.

"Ooohhh . . . you so nice," Soka said, "but my niece have too many job today. Take care kid, mow the lawn, study."

Sundara sensed him looking to her for help, interpretation, anything, but it was no use. The situation was past all hope now. She couldn't even meet his eyes.

"Okay." He started for the door. "Nice to meet you," he said, sounding defeated. "See you at school, Sundara."

She stood rooted to the spot, her good-bye barely audible.

CHAPTER 11

The door had hardly closed behind him before Soka turned on her.

"So! When the cat's away, the mouse becomes king!"

Sundara shrank from her.

"I can't believe you'd deceive me this way. You *knew* this was wrong. A boy in our house!"

"Please, Younger Aunt." She backed up as Soka advanced, the boys scuttling behind her to the safety of the family room. "It was a mistake. I—"

"And then I find you've been sneaking off with him too."

"Only once," Sundara whispered. "And we haven't done anything wrong."

"Not wrong, she says. Sneaking off isn't wrong?"
"Yes, I suppose it is, but I meant that we hadn't—"
"The way it looks is bad enough. Don't you understand? If people hear you're becoming an American brat, I will never find you a good husband. Shame! What a way to repay us for taking care of you! Ungrateful little crocodile!"

Sundara's throat closed painfully against welling tears. Did Soka have to deliver this tirade in front of the boys?

"Oh, I want to die when I think how I told the wife of Pok Sary her stories couldn't possibly be true."

Sundara's head jerked up. *The wife of Pok Sary?*

"Yes, that's right. You'd better look scared. I heard about your sitting alone with some white skin at school. I tried to ignore this since it came from her, and you know how she envies us. And see what I get for trusting you? You've made me look like a fool. Ah, this would tear your mother's heart, to see how you speak from the palm of your hand, then give me the back of it."

Sundara braced herself against the dining room table. Why had she ever done such a thing? Risked the very roof over her head? Jonathan's persuasive smiles already seemed a distant memory.

"You're supposed to be *studying* at school. You have a chance for the kind of education the higher classes have always wanted for their children. So what do you do? Start flirting with American boys!"

"We only talked," Sundara pleaded.

"But don't you see? This is the way it starts. Just talking. Forget American boys. Do you want to be married and divorced, over and over? You deserve better. Hold yourself above this, Niece. You must marry the Khmer way."

Part of her longed to beg for Soka's sympathy, make her see how hard it was to keep the old ways when you were young. But the longer Soka scolded, the feebler Sundara's excuses seemed, even to herself.

"Think about getting a good job, having kids, and taking care of your parents when they grow old."

"Yes, Younger Aunt," Sundara murmured. But would her parents have the chance to grow old?

"No good can come from going with Americans. Oiee! Didn't you see on the news? One refugee stabbed another over the most pitiful-looking white girl. And neither was even the father of her baby? This is what it leads to!"

"But Younger Aunt," Sundara said, summoning her nerve, "what has that to do with us? Jonathan is the son of a doctor."

"Son of a doctor, son of a President Carter. It makes no difference."

"But not just any doctor." Sundara took a deep breath. "The doctor who saved Pon. Dr. McKinnon."

Surprise softened Soka's face. "The son of a good family, then." She looked toward the door where he'd just gone out, as if wishing she could now recall him for closer inspection. She peered at Sundara, intrigued in spite of herself. "And this son of Dr. McKinnon, he's truly fond of you?" In the instant before Sundara could reply, Soka frowned away her curiosity as inappropriate. "But then, *his* feelings are not our concern. Their ways are not our ways. Even with a good family, he is not good for you. You must not think of him anymore. You must forget him."

The words Soka demanded caught in Sundara's throat.

Soka glared. "You will forget him."

Sundara placed her palms together at her forehead in obedience. "I will forget him."

This humble promise seemed to reduce the last embers of Soka's anger to ashen weariness. "Niece, can't you see how hard this is for me?" She sighed. "You're my responsibility. I'm supposed to make sure you grow up properly." She glanced at the door. "Naro and his mother saw the boy's car. Don't expect me to hide the dying of an elephant with a tea tray."

With that she took her forgotten shopping list from the counter and abandoned Sundara to the wide eyes of her cousins. Sundara sank into a chair at the table, burying her head in her arms. She'd imagined this fearful scene so many times; now it had finally come true.

"Ravy," she said after a few minutes, "must you stand there looking at me that way?"

She pushed herself up and dropped to the mat on the kitchen floor. Sitting cross-legged, she resumed shucking the corn.

"Sundara?" Ravy edged over.

She stared at his Adidas, his bare, bony knees. "Yes?"

He rubbed his ankle with the toe of his other shoe, then squatted. "I like Jonathan McKinnon too."

She swallowed hard at this unexpected sympathy. "Thank you, Ravy. That's nice of you." She tore the green husks from a cob. "It's such a beautiful day. Why don't you turn off the TV and go play outside?"

"We will, when the game's over."

He left her alone then. She'd be outside in a minute if she were Ravy. Just imagine. Right now Jonathan was driving along somewhere, the wind in his hair. What would that have felt like, riding with him? Free, that's how, like having wings . . .

Oh, what a sea of trouble. Better if she'd never spoken

to Jonathan, never made a place in her heart for him. Now that place would be so empty.

Her own mother might have been more understanding, she thought with a pang, the kind to consider her daughter's happiness, arrange a marriage with a boy she already liked. But maybe Soka was right. Perhaps her mother would also be enraged at this, might come someday and weep at her wickedness.

It was hard to know what her mother would be like now. It hurt Sundara to admit it even to herself, but sometimes she could not clearly recall her mother's face. Not with a loving expression, anyway.

If only so many of her last looks had not been angry ones. "You foolish child," she'd said. "There's no room to be dragging a parasol along on the plane. What will it take to make you be more practical?"

But her father had intervened. "Oh, let her take it. What can it hurt? The poor child . . ."

"The poor child? What about me? While we all go crazy with this awful shelling, all she can do is whine about having to stay home! I come back from the market after risking my life to get our food and here she is, complaining, on and on . . ."

Sundara shut her eyes now. If only they had known it was the last time they would see each other. . . .

When the doorbell rang, Sundara's heart began to pound. Jonathan? He wouldn't dare come back, would he? But it was Moni standing there.

"Oh, Moni, I'm so glad you've come." She hurried her into the house. "You will not believe what just happened. It still seems like a bad dream."

"Tell me, Little Sister." Moni automatically settled

herself on the mat to help with the corn. No use in idle hands.

Leaning forward, Sundara related the whole incident, trying to keep her voice low. It would not do for the boys to hear her complaining about their mother.

"Actually, I'm lucky she didn't throw me out," she concluded, then added matter-of-factly, "She hates me, you realize."

"Hates you? You're her own niece. How can she hate you?"

Sundara pressed her lips together. "She has her reasons."

Moni frowned. "Sometimes you talk crazy."

"It was so foolish of me to risk making her mad like this. Even when I am perfectly obedient I can't please her. So what could I expect from lying about Jonathan? And to be truthful, I am angry with him, too. I can't understand why he would *do* this. To come here to our house! Maybe I should have been rude and not let him in. I've told him before that Khmer girls can't be alone with boys, but I don't think he ever believes me. He just laughs. And then, today . . . You know the way Americans always pat the children's heads? He did that to Pon!"

"No!"

"Yes! So when Soka came back, Pon runs right up to her: 'Mother, the white man touched my head. Am I going to be stupid now?'"

Moni's eyes went wide. "Do you think he will be?"

"Moni!" Sundara lowered the cob she held. "Haven't you noticed? The Americans do this all the time. It doesn't hurt."

"But perhaps American children are different. Maybe their souls are lodged elsewhere."

"We are all humans, aren't we? We're not *that* different. Anyway, whether it actually harms them isn't the point, is it? The point is, our people don't like it. So his doing it didn't help things one bit." She threw down a cob, took up another ear. "Now Soka says I must have nothing to do with him."

"That will be hard for you."

"Yes, it will. Oh, Moni, if only she knew him. She thinks American boys are all bad, but Jonathan's really very kind and sensitive, not a loud, brawling type at all. He's been so nice to me. He's made me feel alive again. Oh, why didn't I stop seeing him long ago? Now it will be like I die."

Moni shook her head sympathetically. They worked in silence for a while.

At last Moni spoke again. "With all your troubles," she ventured, "it doesn't seem quite right to tell my happy news."

Sundara's head snapped up. "Moni! You and Chan Seng are going to be married!" She searched her friend's face. "Did I guess right?"

Moni smiled. "As soon as the stars are studied to choose a lucky day."

"Oh Moni, that's wonderful. Please forgive my rudeness, going on and on about my own problems." Joy laced with envy filled Sundara. "Tell me about it. Will you have a traditional ceremony?" She thought of the first wedding she ever attended, the wedding of Naro and Soka. How beautiful Soka had looked dressed in shimmering gold silk, her eyes outlined in black.

"Yes, traditional, but not as fancy as if we were back home. I hope you will all come."

"Don't worry, no one will want to miss a feast. Will

you be renting your clothes up in Portland?" It would be lovely to see Moni as a Khmer bride, especially after never having seen her in anything but castoffs from the church people.

"I haven't even decided that yet. We have a lot of plans to make in a hurry!" The pile of shucked corn grew higher as Moni told how Chan Seng had found a better-paying janitorial job and planned to take more classes at the community college, how they were going to try selling spring rolls at the county fairs next summer, how they hoped to get an apartment in a complex where other Khmers lived. "I'm so happy," she concluded. "Now I will truly have a place of my own. I will be a wife."

"I'm happy for you too." If not the most exciting future, at this moment it sounded wonderfully secure. A home of her own. "I wonder if things will ever work out so well for me. I suppose it *would* be easier to marry another Khmer."

"Easier than what?"

"Than . . . than marrying an American, I guess." Sundara's cheeks grew warm as she realized what she'd been thinking. "One thing I don't understand, Moni. If it's good to marry a Chinese so your children will have light skin, why isn't it even better to marry a white man?"

Moni looked puzzled. "I never thought of that."

"Of course, I think judging people by their skin color is foolish to begin with, don't you?"

"Well," Moni said, always honest, "I think lighter skin *is* prettier."

"I suppose so," Sundara admitted. "But only because that's what I've been taught. I don't think it should be that way. Besides, it's not the color of skin that makes people different. I'm doing a report for school on a country called

Northern Ireland. You should see how they're fighting there—white against white."

"Can this be true?"

"Yes! And look at our homeland—Khmer killing Khmer. So I don't think color is everything." She sighed. "Still, when it comes to marriage, I suppose it's easier when both are of the same race." She hesitated, then decided to risk a confession. "Did I ever tell you I was as good as promised to a boy at home?"

"No, really?"

"Yes, his name was Chamroeun. I haven't heard anything about him since we left. He lived down the street from us in Phnom Penh. Such fun we had. He was very handsome, I remember. I wonder what he looks like now. He would be nineteen or twenty."

"If he's still alive."

Sundara glanced up, shocked. "Of course he's alive."

Moni bit her lip. "I'm sorry. I don't mean to sadden you, but you did just mention all the killing . . ."

"Oh, but it's different with Chamroeun." She forced her voice to be light, as if her friend's words had not shaken her. "He was so clever. And such a smile. He could talk his way out of anything. It was he who taught my brother all his tricks, how to wheedle money from my mother for treats from the vendor. Fried banana, that was our favorite." Sundara smiled at the memory, then sighed. "I've listed his name along with those of my family and other friends in my letters to the Thai camps. Soka knows nothing of him, though."

"Ah, that reminds me. I've been thinking that with so many escaping Kampuchea, someone might have news of my family, my little baby girl. Could you help me with a letter to be posted in the camps? I can't write very well, as you know."

"Of course," Sundara said, "but are you prepared for all the letters you will get? If it is known you are in the United States, you will receive piles of letters from people you don't even know, asking you for money for food, for guns—"

"For guns?"

"Yes, for the resistance fighters. We get letters all the time. At first we tried to help everyone—a little American money lasts a long time there. But Soka says she doesn't want to pay for more guns. She says you never know who the bullets might hit. So finally we realized we could help only a few to buy food."

"Better to help a few than none at all."

"Yes, but oh, it makes you cry in your heart to read their sad pleas and not be able to do anything."

"I must send the letter, though. I can't really rest until I learn what happened to my little one. You see, every time I hear a story about a family escaping with their baby, I think, why didn't I bring mine out? At the time, I thought leaving her was the right thing to do, but now . . ."

"Oh Moni, please don't blame yourself. What about all the stories where a family was caught by the Khmer Rouge because a baby cried? I'm sure you did the right thing."

"Maybe," Moni said, but it was clear that like every other Khmer in America, she could not seem to rid her heart of the what-ifs.

After they finished with the corn, they composed the letter.

"I have a feeling this will work," Moni said, her brave and optimistic self again. "I think that finally fortune is smiling on me."

Will I ever have such a chance for happiness? Sundara wondered, closing the door after Moni. Maybe so, if only she and Chamroeun could find each other again. And they would, no matter what Moni said. Hadn't he promised it that last night in Phnom Penh?

The air had been hot and still, no breath of breeze. Sleepless, she'd heard muffled voices from the garden. Rising from her wooden bed, she'd drawn aside her mosquito netting, crept to the window, and unlatched the shutter. Against the black sky, red fires glowed on the horizon. Peering through the window bars, down through the lacy leaves of the jacaranda, she made out the figures of her brother and . . . it was Chamroeun!

Hastily she rewrapped her sarong and smoothed her hair, eyeing her little sister. Mayoury slept soundly inside her netting, undisturbed by the far-off boom of artillery that had become so much a part of their lives. Sundara crept past her, bare feet silent on the polished wood floor. The little scamp would surely tattle if she woke up. Holding her breath, Sundara slipped into the hall. In the main room she could hear her parents speaking in low tones. She tiptoed through the cooking room, down the back steps, and picked her way across the parched and dusty yard.

"Who's there?" came Samet's hoarse whisper.

"Shh! It's only me, Brother."

"Sundara! You're not supposed to be out of the house. Especially with the curfew."

"Don't you start bossing me too!"

"Well, you're going to get in trouble. Mother's annoyed with you enough as it is."

"So what? Since I'm leaving tomorrow, what difference will it make? I had to say good-bye to Chamroeun, didn't I?"

"Ah, so they finally managed to get the plane ticket, then," Chamroeun said. "Good."

"Oh? So you don't want me around anymore, either, is that it?" Sundara showed him her dimples, waiting to see that smile of his in return.

But Chamroeun was not in a joking mood. "The Communists control the river now," he said. "Everyone says the end is coming soon. Phnom Penh is not a good place for you to be."

Sundara's stomach began to flutter. She had always trusted his judgment. If he thought the city was about to be overrun, perhaps there was truth in the rumor.

"You know, Samet," he said. "younger than we are being sent to fight. I'm thinking of joining up."

"But Chamroeun!" Now Sundara was truly alarmed. "I don't want you to get hurt or killed." *Boys!* Why were they always so eager to fight?

"Don't worry about me," Chamroeun said, his hand going to the cylinder of rolled gold he wore around his neck. "My father had the One Who Knows prepare this *katha* with my own charmed words engraved inside. Nothing can hurt me as long as I wear it. But *you*, Sundara . . . nothing could save a pretty girl like you from the Khmer Rouge."

"Don't talk that way!" she protested, the prickling of fear contending with joy. Chamroeun had called her pretty!

"It's true, Sister. Haven't you heard the rumors? When the Khmer Rouge soldiers capture a young girl, they—"

"For the love of heaven!" Chamroeun interrupted. "Don't tell her! Girls should not even have to imagine such things."

"Please don't run off to be a soldier," Sundara begged him. "If you were gone when I came back, I couldn't bear it. Say you won't do it, or I don't want to go!"

A screaming shell split the night. Sundara tensed. *Boom! Boom-boom!*

"Ahh!" Samet breathed. "That one sounded closer."

Boldly, Sundara seized Chamroeun's hands. "I'm frightened for you when you talk of fighting. I'm afraid we'll never see each other again. Never in this life."

"Better that than to have you fall into the hands of the Khmer Rouge." Seeing her terror, he softened his voice. "But don't worry, Pretty One." He smiled. "I will come find you wherever you are. Someday when the war's over."

He had sounded so confident that night, of *course* she believed him. Chamroeun could make her believe anything. Remembering his smile now, she knew it was true. Someday he'd come.

And until that day, the wonderful day when she stood at the airport and watched her handsome, grown-up Chamroeun step off the plane, she would just have to wait faithfully. And surely being faithful did not mean involving herself with an American boy. Shame. Was this the way to honor Chamroeun after the promise he'd made?

She would see Jonathan no more. But how to tell him? The next time she was to meet him, she decided, she would simply not be there. That would be the least painful, most face-saving way for both of them. When she didn't come to the courtyard at break on Monday, he would surely understand, without her saying so, that their meetings must end.

Wouldn't he?

CHAPTER 12

Pretending she didn't see Jonathan hurrying down the hall, she stooped at her open locker, primly looped braids swinging forward.

"Hey, what's wrong?" he said, puffing a little. "Why'd you take off so fast after international relations?"

She stood up slowly.

"And you weren't in the courtyard at break."

She still didn't meet his eyes. "I'm thinking it would be better this way."

"What way? What are you talking about?" He leaned against the lockers.

"I'm sorry, but it's better for everyone, I think, if we don't see each other anymore."

"*Sundara.*" He stood upright. "You don't mean that. You can't."

She frowned. "I think you make this difficult." She glanced around; she didn't want anyone watching. "I don't want to talk so hard, but like I tell you so many time, in my country a girl doesn't go out with a boy. That the reason I'm in so much trouble."

"But you've never gone out with me. How can you be in trouble?"

She sighed. It was so hard to explain.

"Does this have something to do with Saturday? Me coming to your house?"

She nodded. "They very angry I let you inside."

"Oh, come *on* . . ."

"And then when you mention about the sailing . . ." She trailed off, shaking her head, still unable to believe the magnitude of his blunder.

"But that's so unfair! I mean, I'm sorry I don't read sign language or eye language or whatever it is I'm too much of an American clod to pick up on, but I was trying to say the right thing. You're always saying how important families are, right? So I thought if I mentioned mine she'd at least realize I wasn't just some lone punk cruising the streets."

"But it was a secret. They don't know I go with you. They would never allow it."

"A one hundred percent chaperoned family outing? You have to sneak out for something like that?"

She started walking down the hall. He followed.

"If it was such a terrible thing to do, why'd you do it?"

She stopped and faced him, hurt. "Now you're mad with me because I'm risking a lot of trouble to be with you?"

He reached to touch her shoulder, but she backed away, notebook for a shield. "Even I like you," she said softly, "some thing that are okay for you are not okay for me. I must follow the wish of my family."

He shifted from one foot to the other and looked down the hall away from her. In the silence between them, she heard the dull hum of voices, the clinking of dishes from the cafeteria. The bell rang.

"I must go," she said.

"No, don't. We've got to get this straight."

"Jonatan . . ."

"Mostly it's just because I'm white, right? Your aunt would like me better with black hair and brown eyes."

"It's not just the color. You see, if you are Khmer, you would not ask me to go out with you in the first place."

"Will you stop making that sound like such a crime? I can't believe all this is happening because I asked to take you for one lousy drive in broad daylight."

She sighed. "You see why I rather not talk about this? America is *your* country. You know how to act here. It's not right for me to tell you."

"Just tell me why two people can't . . . be friends."

"I don't know. I only know we are taught that our elders know best."

"But they don't! Not this time. Can't you see that?"

"Jonatan! I don't like it you make me talk this way and argue. I warn you many time about this."

"I know, I know." He shook his head. "I guess I just never figured you'd try so hard to stick to your old customs now that you're here. I thought you wanted to be more American."

"I *do*, but I must obey my aunt and uncle."

"But you're *not* in Cambodia anymore."

She narrowed her eyes at him. "You think I need you to tell me this?"

He sighed. "I'm sorry. But the whole thing makes me so mad. It's so unfair. Why should you be in trouble? You haven't done anything wrong. God, compared to most of the girls I know—"

A picture of Cathy flickered through her mind. Cathy, with her hand in the back pocket of his jeans . . .

"What am I supposed to do? Just let you walk away? Oh, well, I didn't care about her anyway—"

"Jonatan . . ." She never dreamed he'd be so upset, make such a scene. "You have everything. You don't need me and all my sad story."

"But I *do*."

Heaven help her, if she let herself look into those eyes any longer, she'd be giving in again. "This is bad for both of us," she said. "I think now they right in the beginning. When you ask me will I eat lunch with you, I should say no. Then we wouldn't have a hurt like this now."

"But Sundara—"

She began to back away. "No use to argue! Too late. They make me promise." She took a breath that burned her lungs. "They make me promise I never talk to you again."

She turned and pushed blindly into the girls' room, her heart thudding.

CHAPTER 13

Holding her braid wound on top of her head, she stood under the hot shower, eyes closed, still uneasy with this American school custom of forcing everyone to shower together after gym class. She didn't want to see other people naked. She'd grown up with warnings against even looking at *herself* naked. "You must cover your body in the shower," her mother always said. "It's better that way." And these customs were hard to break. Look at Soka. Even now, in an American bathroom with a lock on the door, wearing a sarong to shower all by herself! Sundara had given up that part of it easily enough, but she would never get used to an audience.

Opening her eyes, she inadvertently caught a glimpse

of Cathy Gates through the steam clouds. Those tan lines of hers! Did she really wear a bathing suit so tiny? Sundara shut her eyes again.

It had been hard, these last weeks, seeing the American girl walking the halls with Jonathan once again. Cathy seemed to have everything. This was *her* country, *her* language, and most of all, Jonathan was *her* boyfriend. She always looked like a girl in one of those Coke ads on television.

But Sundara could tell Jonathan wasn't so satisfied.

Once, in the hall at school, their eyes had met. Before she glanced away, she caught the flicker of embarrassment in his, an apology. Another time he'd followed her, tried to talk.

"Just let me explain . . ."

"Explain?"

"About Cathy."

"Jonatan, you don't have to explain anything to me. That not my business." And resolutely she'd turned away. No use fighting Cathy Gates for a boy she couldn't have anyway.

Another time, as she was leaving the post office after mailing a package to Valinn, she'd run into Mrs. McKinnon just inside the door.

"Sundara!" Mrs. McKinnon stopped shaking the rain from her umbrella. "What a nice surprise." Then she cocked her head, her eyebrows going together in a way that saddened her smile. "We were hoping we'd get to see more of you."

"Ohh . . ." Sundara watched the last leaves trembling on a tree beyond the glass doors.

Mrs. McKinnon waited, then spoke hesitantly. "Sundara, I— Maybe this is none of my business, but did something happen between you and Jonathan?"

Sundara glanced at her through lowered lashes. "He doesn't tell you?"

She frowned. "Tell me what?"

Sundara stared at the marble-tiled floor. "My family won't let me be with him."

"Oh. I see. No, he didn't say anything." She straightened her stack of manila envelopes. "Is it—do they not want you to date whites?"

Sundara bit her lip. "I cannot date anyone. It is— Oh, I feel so bad. Your family so nice to me. And then my family—"

"No, no, no, now . . . Don't you worry about that. We understand." Then she sighed, shifting her umbrella and envelopes, pulling her purse strap up over her shoulder. "I knew *something* was eating at him, the way he's been dragging around lately. . . ."

Don't think about it, Sundara scolded herself now, taking a towel from the stack on her way out of the shower. He'd get over it. He'd forget all about her before long.

She should be ashamed, letting him put his arm around her that way, allowing him to untie her hair. Chamroeun might not want to marry her if he knew of this.

How she ached to have once again all that was rightfully hers. The boy promised to her. Her own land and people, the customs that had been passed down for centuries. Maybe she should ask Soka if she could study the traditional royal ballet here, in the new land, dance at the statewide New Year's celebration in a golden-spired head-dress. The trips to Portland for lessons would require time and money, it was true, but maybe Soka would think it worth the cost, to have everyone see Sundara making graceful poses next to the daughter of Pok Sary, her niece no longer excluded from this upper-class tradition as she would have been at home.

Sundara only wanted something of her own. Why hadn't she paid more attention when her parents tried to pass it all on to her? Why hadn't she listened when they visited the ancient temples at Angkor? "Look at this, children," her father had said over and over. "Remember what is carved in these stones: 'Of the qualities acquired, the highest is knowledge.' " She and Samet had obediently read every temple inscription he pointed out to them, but Sundara could think only what a bore it was, having to be solemn under the unseeing eyes of the huge stone faces. The esplanade seemed made for running, the twisting hallways and inner chambers perfect for hide-and-seek. What a lighthearted child she'd been. How little she'd understood of religion, of the world and war. . . .

After school, the rowdy boys on the bus shoved each other and sent wads of paper whizzing past her as she gazed out at the gray sky. The sun now seemed something only dimly remembered from the past, and it was easy to believe there had never been any lunches under the trees with Jonathan, no sailing on the lake. She sighed. Just as well, perhaps. Her only thought now must be to remain true to the ways of the Khmers, become a doctor and help people. And when she married, it would be in the Khmer way, with a beautiful ceremony like that of Moni and Chan Seng.

How happy they had looked together in their rented silks—like ancient royalty. Moni had never been prettier, and slimmer, too, having confided to Sundara that at last she felt sure of having enough to eat. It was a lovely party, a pleasant respite from the gloom of so many recent Khmer gatherings.

Soka had even surprised Sundara with a length of silvery blue silk to wear. Why would she do such a thing? Silk was expensive in America. They couldn't raise the worms and spin it themselves as they had at home. The kind they liked had to be sent from Thailand. Why would Soka bestow such a treasure on her?

All week after the wedding Sundara had been imagining herself in rustling bridal clothes, resting on the ceremonial pillows, her wrist bound to that of her groom with a silken cord. And when she shyly smiled up at him, the man she pictured was, of course, Chamroeun. She tried to bring this vision to mind each time she saw Jonathan and Cathy together. It helped.

Now, stepping off the bus, she flipped up the hood of her new jacket. Deep down she longed for Kampuchea every day of her life, but winter always made the longing worse. She'd grown up with only two seasons: warm-dry and warm-wet. Here, in the cold-wet of an Oregon November, you could not even hold your head up. The rain had a way of beating you down, making you hunch your shoulders and feel the spiteful heavens were trying to break your spirit, opening up on you alone, even though plainly it poured on everyone.

Once the heavy leaden clouds began rolling over the Coast Range mountains in the last weeks of October, the rain never seemed to stop. Naro's fretting that the constant dampness was sure to rot the strange soft wood of their American-style house was bad enough, but Grandmother's mutterings were worse. "Someone must have died last week," she kept saying, listening to the drops drumming on the windows. "Now they are weeping because they realize they are dead." Maybe so. You had only to turn on the TV to know that enough Khmers were dying to flood the earth with tears from heaven.

Magazine covers showed hollow-eyed Cambodian children; television networks carried nightly film reports of the sick and starving refugees dragging themselves across the Kampuchean border to Thailand in the wake of the Vietnamese invasion.

Even people at school were becoming aware of the situation. Once in a while a sympathetic classmate would ask Sundara if she'd seen the news. And while Mrs. Cathcart never mentioned it directly, she did ask Sundara how things were going in a way that made it clear she understood how difficult this must be for her.

Now the bus pulled away with a blast of stinking diesel exhaust. Sundara stepped off the curb into a puddle. *Ye! Chambaue!* She pulled back her foot, cold and soaked. If only she could get some decent boots. Maybe next year . . . Oh, Soka was right. How ungrateful. She finally had her plum-colored jacket and what difference did it make? Already she was wanting something else. Shameful, fretting about a little thing like wet feet when people were suffering their lives away in Kampuchea.

At home, the grown-ups whispered about it all the time, falling silent when Sundara and the boys drew near, wanting to shield them. But they couldn't resist gathering around the TV each night.

Sundara had heard all the Khmer Rouge horror stories before, the forced-labor camps, the brutal massacres. But now these tales came not just from an escapee here or there, but from every one of thousands upon thousands of refugees, the stories varying only in the specific details of suffering. *Genocide*, they were calling it. The killing of a people.

Sundara and her family stared at the screen images of spindly children, weak with hunger and exhaustion, some of them newly orphaned. Soka would cry; Naro clutched the amulet around his neck; the boys watched round-eyed, uncomprehendingly. They knew these were Khmers who were dying, their own people, but they did not feel it as Grandmother did. Naro sometimes urged the old woman to go in the other room, but she insisted on watching. "We can never go home," she would moan. "My bones will be scattered in this foreign land, and how will my spirit ever find its way to be reborn?"

Once again the ghosts of starving children haunted Sundara's dreams. She saw their faces, their rolled-back eyes, felt their limp, skeletal weightlessness in her arms as she fought her way through crowds of people, stepping over dead bodies whose bony fingers snatched at her ankles. Come back, they wailed. Come back . . . But she kept running, heart pounding. *Hurry*, get away, *far* away . . . Then, just when she'd made it to safety, just when she had taken her first easy breath, she'd open her *krama* and find the child inside shattering into ghastly flakes, hot ashes rising in a whirlwind. Her mouth would open in a dry scream. Noooo! *Nooooooo!* She'd lurch awake, burning, a sick thudding in her chest. . . .

Now, taking off her wet shoes in the covered entry alcove, she noticed Soka's white work Nikes on the mat. They were not neatly paired as usual but askew, one on its side. Lining them up properly, Sundara wondered what her aunt was doing home already.

"Oh, Niece," Soka cried, opening the door, "the news is bad, very bad." She pulled Sundara inside.

"What, something on the television? Why have you come home?"

"I was so upset after lunch they told me to leave work. You see, I came home for the mail and look, letters from the camps. You don't remember this family, but we knew them in Réam. They escaped to Thailand. Oh, it makes me cry in my heart, all the people the Communists have massacred. Whole families, she says. Even the babies."

Grisly scenes rose in Sundara's mind. She braced for the worst.

"Oiee! They say my good friend Theary—she and her family, all killed. I last saw her sitting on her steps the afternoon we left. Ah, Theary! Why didn't you come with us? I wish I could have convinced her."

"But Younger Aunt, *please*, what of our family? Was there news of them?"

"No, no. Nothing about family. Thank God we can still have hope for them. Ah, but Theary! Remember her sitting there as we passed going down to the ship?"

"I'm not sure, Younger Aunt." Sundara was trying to breathe again. No bad news of her family! Just the thought of it had dizzied her. What if bad news ever actually came?

"Don't you remember?" Soka pressed her, as if somehow Sundara's memory of her last parting with Theary could alter the outcome. "Why, I *begged* her to come with us."

"Yes, of course," Sundara said, remembering only her

aunt's own screaming protests at being forced to leave. What tricks one's memory could play.

"Oiee! Your letter is sad, too, I'm afraid. I opened it thinking it might tell about your mother. I'm grateful it's not bad news of her, it's not family. But still, it's sad. Someone who lived on your street."

The blood drained to Sundara's feet, her head tingled. She took the smudged paper in trembling hands, but before she could focus on the Khmer script, Soka summed it up:

"Someone you knew named Chamroeun is dead."

CHAPTER 14

Sundara sat in international relations class, watching her hand fill line after line with notes about South Africa's apartheid policy, her mind struggling with the cold and final truth: Her wrist would never be bound to Chamroeun's in the ceremonial red cord of a Khmer wedding; never again in this life would she gaze upon his smiling face. *Never.* This was the cruel end to which all her hoping had come, a blow that had been poised above her unknowing neck like a heavy sword for four long years.

She stared, unseeing, at the blackboard. If Chamroeun had been dead all this time, shouldn't she have known it in her heart? Shouldn't she have felt it? In the long day since she'd learned of his death, only one small measure of comfort had come to her: Chamroeun's fate could not possibly be her punishment for allowing herself to care for Jonathan, as she had imagined in her first, guilty grief. Now, calmer, she reminded herself that Chamroeun had been killed long before she'd looked up to find Jonathan's blue eyes upon her.

When the bell rang, she headed straight for her locker and dumped her books. She couldn't eat lunch today; she wasn't sure she ever wanted to eat again. She put on her jacket, went out, and started across the patio.

"Sundara?"

Startled, she looked back. It was Jonathan, at the open cafeteria door.

"Hey, where you going? It's raining."

She didn't answer, just turned and kept walking. She heard his shoes slapping behind her on the wet pavement.

"Something's happened, hasn't it?"

She stared at the dull gray sky. "You going to get wet."

"I don't care. Look, you're good at hiding it, Sundara, but I know you. You've got to tell me what's going on." He took her arm. "Come on, I know where we can talk alone."

She felt too weak to protest. What did it matter anyway? They skirted the cafeteria wing and he led her through the gap in the chain link fence, jumping the puddle that filled the worn spot. "Look out," he warned, but she slogged straight through. They made their way across the soggy football field toward the covered bleachers, Sundara squishing one foot in front of the other, not caring. The rain stung her cheeks, plastered her jeans to her thighs. Finally they reached the bleachers, where he sat her down on a splintery bench.

She shoved her hands in her pockets and hunched her

shoulders against the chill. She knew he was waiting, but the words didn't want to come.

"Can't you tell me?"

Finally she spoke, her voice flat and lifeless. "It about Chamroeun."

"Oh." He looked out over the football field. "What about him?"

"Yesterday I get a letter. . . . He dead."

Jonathan turned. "Oh no."

She nodded, biting her lip. "He die when he only sixteen, not much older than I last see him. They kill for steal a potato. Can you believe? He so hungry he get up in the night to find a peel and for that they chop his neck with a hoe."

Jonathan's face . . . She'd told too much, been too blunt. Americans didn't want to hear about heads getting chopped off. . . .

"The Khmer Rouge?"

She nodded. "Pol Pot men." She clenched her teeth. "Chamroeun—if he looking from heaven, he so mad. If he gonna die, he want to die fighting, not be kill like—"

"Shh!" Jonathan whispered, putting his arms around her. For a moment she stayed rigid, then she sank against him, her dry sobs vibrating from her body through his.

"I see now, this the way it will be." Her words were muffled in the damp flannel of his shirt. "Before, I have hope, but now it starts. Now I will learn that everybody I love die."

"Maybe not, Sundara. Maybe . . ."

"Mayoury. I worry so much about little Mayoury." She pulled back. "How can she live if Chamroeun cannot? He the clever one. All the people who run away from Cambodia, now they can tell the world the true. When

they marching everybody out of Phnom Penh, they say
the little one the first to die. Then they killing all over the
place, for no reason. Make you watch your mother die,
and if a tear slip out, okay, that's it, you die too. The letters we get . . . Jonatan, they kill a baby for a game!
They—"

"Don't, Sundara."

She stopped. "Too terrible? You cannot hear?"

"No. I mean, yes, it's too terrible, but . . . Please,
don't think about it. It won't do any good. You're going to
make yourself sick."

She stared at all the initials inked and scratched into
the wooden bench below them. In looping red letters
someone had written, *Smile! God loves us!*

"Look here. This hard to believe. Where is God when
they killing the children?" She laughed bitterly. "Oh,
maybe this person just mean God love Americans. He not
watching in Cambodia."

"Sundara. I've never heard you talk like this before."

She bit her lip. "I never know everybody dying before." She let her clasped hands fall between her knees and
turned her face up to the sky, eyes squeezed tight. "I wish
I die with them. I wish I never leave."

"Don't say that!" He took her by the shoulders. "What
good would it do? And anyway, why do you keep blaming
yourself when you didn't have any choice?"

"But I did! I never tell you this before. I even tell
myself they make me come. But I could have gone back!
Some did. One of the ship goes back to the shore. Anyone
who change his mind can get on, but I don't go, because
I'm afraid."

"But that was the right thing."

"No, no, my parents—"

"Your parents must have been glad to think you got away."

"What about my duty to them? I didn't have the courage . . ."

"Right. It didn't take any guts at all to get on a boat and come halfway around the world." He paused. "You're about the bravest person I know."

"You too nice to me. *Brave* is a word for Moni. Not me. You don't understand. I make a promise to my mother . . ." Should she tell? Could she risk it? No, for what if *he* began to hate her too? "Oh, I am nothing but trouble since the day I step on the boat. So why does God spare me?" She searched his face. "You think He spare to punish?"

"No, no . . . that's crazy."

"But sometime I think I must be a very bad person in my last life."

"Come on. Maybe you were a good person. Maybe that's why you were spared. Or maybe because you're special in this life. Maybe God or Fate or whatever has plans for you, like you're supposed to become a doctor. Instead of feeling guilty, why not just assume you're *supposed* to be alive?"

If only she could believe that. But how could she ever feel good about being a survivor when Soka's baby had died?

"And anyway," Jonathan said, "you keep talking like you're this terrible person because you chose the wrong fork in the road. But your uncle knew the score with the Communists. He never would have let you go back. You know that."

Sundara hung her head. He was probably right. Yet perhaps she'd feel better now if she'd tried.

They sat quietly for a few minutes, Sundara staring across the football field, Jonathan watching her.

Finally she broke the silence. "I wonder why the American always think of life like a road. 'Down the road of life,' they like to say."

"Well, it beats talking about the Football Field of Life. That's Coach Hackenbruck's favorite."

She gazed into the distance, no longer seeing the field, the school buildings. "We think of life more like a river. Think of it that way, maybe you right I have no choice. On a river it is not so simple as just choose which way to go. On a river we try to steer a good course, but all the time we getting swept along by a force greater than ourselves.

"A road can go anywhere," she went on, almost to herself, "and then it stop. But a river never stop. All the river flow together and become one. This is more like life, don't you think so? Because then it begin all over again."

He looked at her. "What I think," he said, "is that you're amazing. How did you even make it to school today? Anybody else would be home crying."

"Oh, I cannot cry."

"Can't cry?"

"I never cry since I leave Cambodia."

"Not in four years?"

She shuddered. "Jonatan, I start to cry, I think maybe I never stop."

CHAPTER 15

When I read the words you wrote
I thought my dying hour had come . . .

The mournful song drifted in as Sundara studied at the
dining room table. Through the doorway she could see
Soka huddled with Grandmother on the living room mats,
the two of them wrapped in afghans to ward off the growing winter chill. As she had for two days now, Soka
twisted in her hands a thin, ragged *krama*, grieving for her
lost friend Theary.

Sundara watched her with a strange feeling of envy.
Maybe it helped, crying it out like that. Over time her
own griefs had solidified into a cold, heavy weight in her

chest, immovable, seemingly permanent. How her heart continued to beat against it, how her lungs were able to draw air, she could scarcely understand. If only she could cry.

Turning back to her book, she shivered and rubbed her arms. Truly a cold season was upon them, in body as well as in spirit.

Naro couldn't keep warm either. Tonight he wore an American-style jacket with his sarong as he sat at the other end of the table doing paperwork.

Over the sea I send my spirit
To hurt your heart with one sad plea . . .

Glancing at Sundara, he finally rose and went into Soka and his mother, lightly touching his wife's shoulder. "This isn't helping, is it, Little Sister?" He shut off the tape deck.

Now they heard the rain slamming the windows.

Naro frowned. "Did Ravy take his raincoat to the game?"

Soka's face registered pained surprise. "I don't know," she whimpered. "Oiee! You see what this has done to me? I'm not even a good mother anymore!"

"Don't worry, Younger Aunt," Sundara called. "I made sure he had it."

Soka's silence left Sundara uneasy. Was she wrong to look after Ravy? Did Soka think she was trying to take over her authority?

Naro gave Sundara a small, reassuring nod before returning to his letter-writing tasks—more patient, ever so polite pleas to the bureaucrats who could help reunite their family, more sorting of the requests for help.

Sundara checked the clock. Ravy should be home soon. He always went to the Friday night games with his friends these days, so Sundara's services were not needed. Besides, she hadn't been allowed anywhere since the day her deceit about Jonathan had been discovered.

When Ravy crept in so quietly a few minutes later, she thought at first it was because he feared to disturb the somber mood in the house. But after greeting his parents and grandmother, he motioned her to the back hall with his eyes.

Glancing at her uncle, she placed a marker in her book and slipped after Ravy into the darkened bedroom Pon and Ravy shared with Grandmother. Pon was already fast asleep in the upper bunk. Behind the blanket that had been hung for Grandmother's privacy, they perched on the edge of her neatly made bed.

"Jonathan McKinnon got hurt in the game!" Ravy whispered in English.

A prickling zipped down the backs of her legs. "What happened?"

"A whole bunch of guys tackled him. Then everybody got up but him."

"He doesn't get up at all?"

Ravy shook his head, the whites of his eyes big in the light from the hall. "I think it's bad. They carried him off on a stretcher and an ambulance took him away. They said on the loudspeakers he was going to the hospital."

Sundara begged him for every detail, made him tell everything he saw several times, as if she might squeeze some reassurance from something he'd forgotten the first time through. But Ravy could offer only the revelation that one of the rally girls had made a scene by running onto the field, and the rumor that Jonathan had hurt his head—neither any comfort at all.

What sleep she got that night was fitful and full of restless dreams about Jonathan and Chamroeun, dreams that made no sense. Only when she'd been awake several minutes did the real significance hit her: For the first time ever, she had been dreaming in English.

Early in the morning she rose and stealthily turned on the kitchen radio. Nothing about Jonathan on the local news. After breakfast, with the excuse of buying notebook paper, she headed for the nearby 7-Eleven's pay phone.

It had stopped raining for the moment, but clouds hung low, holding the smoke of wood stoves close over the houses. She kept to a brisk, worm-dodging pace along the wet sidewalk until she rounded the corner that would put her out of sight of the house. Then she broke into a run, heart pounding, lungs burning with the damp morning air.

Strange, yesterday she'd thought only of Chamroeun and the past, both lost to all hope. But this fear for Jonathan had wrenched her back to the present, sparked her to life again, cut short her private mourning. Did this do Chamroeun dishonor? Heaven protect her, she couldn't help it. She was alive and had to move on. Chamroeun was the past, but Jonathan was right now, and suddenly, right now mattered very much.

At the phone booth she stopped, breathing hard, the dry taste of fear in her mouth. Why had she hurried? Was she so eager for bad news? Two identically dressed girls came out of the 7-Eleven with Slurpees, eyeing her curiously. She probably did look odd, just standing by the phone, staring at nothing. Hands shaking, she unfolded a scrap on which she'd scribbled the hospital's number, dropped a coin in the slot, and punched the numbers.

"Yes," a busy-sounding voice said, "a Jonathan McKinnon has been admitted. Room 4202."

Sundara focused on a puddle of oil, shimmering green and purple on the wet parking lot pavement. "He is hurt?"

A pause. "Are you a family member?"

"No, but I'm—"

"Then I can't release any other information." *Click.*

Sundara set the receiver back in its cradle. She gazed up to the hill at the newly built hospital. She would have to go there and see Jonathan for herself. She would take the car and stop at the hospital on her way to do the grocery shopping.

Later, after lunch, she parked the station wagon in the Willamette Grove Memorial lot, turned off the ignition, and sat for a moment, gathering strength.

A tired man balancing a potted plant trudged up the half-dozen steps to the next parking level. A young woman carried a suitcase for a man on crutches. Up at the main door, a boy helped a white-haired lady with a walker.

Sundara paused as she got out of the car. What if the hospital people yelled at her, told her to go away, only family could visit? The brick and cement building loomed large and foreboding as she approached. Would there be lots of tubes and needles? Bad smells? People moaning in pain? Worst of all, what if Jonathan was badly hurt?

And then, above the glass doors, like a message put there just for her, she read this inscription:

LINDA CREW

HERE,
"AT WHATEVER HOUR YOU
COME YOU WILL FIND LIGHT
AND HELP AND HUMAN KINDNESS."
—ALBERT SCHWEITZER

Tears sprang to her eyes. A sense of peace filled her. A good place, good people inside to put this over the door, to know that people coming here might be feeling scared because they were sick or hurt. Or because they feared for a loved one.

Someday she'd be a doctor. Someday she'd be one of those good people inside, ready to offer help and kindness.

And as for today . . . hadn't Jonathan himself called her brave? Surely if she could get on a boat and come halfway around the world, she could walk into a hospital without trembling.

She stepped up to the glass doors; they opened before her.

Jonathan lay propped against the clean white pillows in a cotton gown. His eyes were closed, but his black lashes rested on cheeks still flushed with health. Tubes and dials hung on the wall and around the complicated bed, but with relief Sundara noted that he didn't seem to be hooked up to any of them.

A football game was in progress on the overhead television, being watched, apparently, by an unseen roommate on the other side of the orange plaid curtain.

"Jonatan?"

"Hmm?" He opened his eyes. They looked bluer than ever next to the sky color of his gown. "Sundara." He

]152[

pushed himself to more of a sitting position. "What are you doing here?"

She smiled. "What you think? I come to see for myself you okay."

His smile was sleepy, happily bewildered. "I thought you'd given up on me."

"Silly." Suddenly she wanted to tousle his hair, a strange longing for a girl taught not to touch the heads of others. "You know that not the way I feel."

She smiled. He smiled back at her. For a long time they just looked at each other.

"So. You are okay?" she asked. "I've been so worried."

"Yeah, I'm okay."

"You have a lot of pain?"

"Only when I move. It's like this horrendous head-ache."

"Then it is true, what Ravy tell me? You hurt your head?"

"Yeah, just a slight concussion, turns out."

"But this is very bad," she said softly, "to be hurt in your head. Jonatan, your head is the place of your soul, your life force. You must take care."

She hadn't realized how good it would feel to be near him again. When they'd huddled together in the grand-stands the day before, she'd been so numb with grief she hadn't even thought about it. But now . . . the television football game, the rattling of carts in the hall, the intercom paging some doctor—everything faded into muffled back-ground noise. She and Jonathan might have been alone in this huge building as they gazed at each other.

"I've stopped seeing stars," he finally offered, grin-ning.

"Stars?"

"I mean, my head's okay."

"Ah, that is good. They don't have to cut anything open?"

"Yow." He winced playfully. "The way you put things sometimes . . ."

"Sorry."

He laughed. "No, nothing cut open. Mostly they're just checking my eyeballs a lot."

"Ooh! I'm glad. Soka say they sometime so quick to cut here."

"So tell me," he said after a moment. "How are *you* doing? I've been worried, too, after yesterday. Even in the middle of the game, all I could think about was the stuff you'd told me."

"I'm okay," she said. She didn't want to think about what had happened to Chamroeun anymore. What good would it do?

Another long silence.

Then Jonathan cleared his throat. "Does your aunt know you're here?"

She shook her head. "They think I'm at the store." She glanced at the big clock on the wall and started to back out the door. "Now I see you not too bad, I better go."

He jerked forward. "No, don't—ow." He eased back, closing his eyes. "I forget. I can't do that." He opened his eyes again. "Just stay a *little* longer?"

"Well . . . okay." She shifted nervously. "But only a minute." The room was warm; she eased out of her jacket. Then she glanced out the open door toward the nurses' station in the middle of the circular ward. "Does your father work at this hospital?"

"Sure, sometimes. It's the only hospital we've got, right?"

"It is a good place, I think. I know this when I see what they put above the door."

"Above the door? What do you mean? Where?"

"At the front of the hospital. You never notice the words? Well, maybe you can look at it sometime. It make me think about your father, how he so kind to us when we first come."

"Okay, I will." He pressed the heels of his hands into his eye sockets. "You should have seen him last night. He and Mom were freaking out in here. He kept grabbing my toes. 'Can you feel that? Can you feel it?' I must've told him ten times I could, but he had to hear it over and over."

"He love you very much. He worried about you."

"I know, I know." He sighed. "And I guess I really am lucky. Did you know that guys have been paralyzed in accidents just like this?"

"Really?" She moved to the side of his bed again. "Maybe this kind of an omen for you."

"Makes you wonder, doesn't it? I mean, talk about getting beat over the head with something."

His roommate turned up the television's volume. Jonathan and Sundara looked up at the screen, little figures scrambling over a bright green background.

"At halftime President Carter was on," Jonathan said, "asking people to send money for the camps in Thailand."

"Oh." For a few hours she'd almost forgotten about the camps, the thousands of miserable people. She'd been too busy worrying about this one person, this Jonathan McKinnon.

A lady wearing a smock wheeled in a cart of flowers and set two or three bouquets on Jonathan's bedside stand.

"Oh, no," Jonathan said. "Flowers? This is embarrassing."

"And these," the lady said, handing him a stack of cards that had evidently been hand-delivered.

"And this," a nurse added, struggling to pull a huge balloon bouquet through the door. Each balloon had a smiley face on it.

Jonathan turned red.

The nurse gave Sundara a funny look. "Visiting hours haven't started yet, have they? Jonathan's only supposed to be seeing family members."

He leaned forward. "She's my sister."

"Now wait a minute . . ."

"Adopted," he added.

The nurse didn't believe him for a minute, Sundara saw, but it didn't matter. For a disarming smile like his, she'd wink at the rules. Frowning in mock disapproval, she handed him the braided ribbons of the balloon bouquet and went out after the lady with the cart.

"How *did* you get in here?" he whispered.

Sundara shrugged, smiling. "I just walk in. Hold my head up like I know where I'm going and nobody stop me."

He smiled. Then he pulled out the bouquet's little card. "I knew it. Cathy." He tossed it aside. "I wish she wouldn't do stuff like this."

Sundara hesitated. "Do you want me to tie it to the bed railing?"

"Huh. What I'd really like is for you to open the window and let it float away."

"But Jonatan, what will she think when she come to see you?"

He sighed. "I know, I don't want to hurt her feelings." He let go of the ribbons and shut his eyes as the balloons rose. "But I hate those smiley faces. You'd think she'd know that by now."

Sundara wasn't sure what to say. They'd never once mentioned Cathy's name, but now that the American girl's spirit hovered between them in this white-walled room, there were things she wanted to know, things she suddenly had to know.

"Jonatan?" She watched the balloons bouncing gently against the ceiling. "Do you love Cathy a lot?"

"Catty," he said. "The way you say it, it comes out Catty."

She gave him a chiding look. "You not answering my question."

"Okay, okay. What was the question? Do I love Cathy." He screwed up his face in exaggerated thought, then shook his head. "I don't know. I thought I did. Or maybe I thought I ought to. But do you realize the kind of stuff she talks to me about?" He sat up. "What do I think of her chances for making homecoming court. Should she get a haircut. When am I going to get some new clothes. Why won't I dress up like a rally girl for their pep skit." He sank back. "I'm not sure if she's changed or it's just me." He paused. "I know *I've* changed. Now that I've known you I'm not the same person anymore. *Nothing's* the same. I mean, I never used to worry much, but now when I read the papers I get so upset, and when the coach makes us actually *pray* before the game, I just want to—"

"Jonatan—now be calm. Don't get excited."

"No, really. I've had it. I'm supposed to pray to win a football game when babies are starving?" He gripped the bed's side rails. "You've changed everything. You've made me see the world isn't all nice sunny little places like Willamette Grove."

She lowered her eyelids. "You happier before I come."

"No! I mean, yes, but it was a different kind of happy. A not-knowing sort of happy. When you're with me I'm happy in a knowing sort of way. It goes deeper." He looked at her, then wearily lowered himself. "I'm probably not making any sense at all."

"I understand what you say, I think." She looked away. "Except about Cathy."

He sighed. "You want to know if I love her." He reached over and tilted Sundara's face toward him. "Ask me a question I can answer. Ask me if I love *you.*"

CHAPTER 16

For the next few days, she wore Jonathan's love like a warm cloak around her. The way he'd just come right out and said it! *I love you, Sundara.* Leaving the hospital in a daze, she had realized she couldn't remember anyone ever saying those words to her before—not even her parents. She liked this American way of being so honest. If she were honest with him . . . No, she mustn't think of it. She was not allowed to love Jonathan McKinnon. Still, whatever happened, it was a wonderful feeling, knowing he loved her.

Then one morning the halls were draped with WEL-COME BACK, JONATHAN banners. When Sundara saw them, her heart began to pound. He was back at school. He was somewhere in the building this very minute. What would they say to each other now?

But by break time she hadn't seen him, and as she headed for her locker, she saw the rally girls taking the banners down.

Puzzled, she slowed to a stroll, watching as the glum-faced girls undid their work.

Cathy spotted her and flounced down a ladder with the end of a banner. "I hope you're happy," she muttered, coming at Sundara. "Jonathan's quitting the team." She sniffed. "But then, that's no surprise to you, is it?"

Streams of people were dividing around them. Sundara caught snatches of the mumbling. *Did you hear? He did? But why?* They sounded dismayed, bewildered.

Cathy gave the other end of the banner a savage yank. "Do you realize you have completely ruined him?" Her voice was low and fury-packed, her eyes red from crying. "He used to be so much fun. And he was happy too. Then you come along—Miss Gloom and Doom—" She wadded the banner and stuffed it in a garbage can. "He hasn't been himself since the day he heard that poem of yours. And I'm not the only one who says so. Everybody's noticed it."

Sundara glanced around, clutching her notebook to her chest. So Jonathan had finally done it. She lowered her eyes and took a deep breath.

"You know, Cathy," she said softly, "before, I'm a little afraid of you. I always think, 'Oh, Cathy Gates, she his girlfriend. She understand him.'" She looked into Cathy's eyes. "But now I see you don't understand his spirit at all."

Cathy crossed her arms over her chest. "And of course you do."

Sundara hesitated. "Maybe."

"By all means, enlighten me."

"Well, you say he not himself. How do you know? Maybe this the real Jonatan now and he not himself before."

"Oh, very clever. Maybe *I* ought to start spouting all this mystical shit. Because that's what he's hung up on. It's not really you at all."

Sundara looked away, cheeks burning. Jonathan loved her. He'd said so.

"I used to feel sorry for you," Cathy went on, "but now I am just so sick of hearing about your deep, dark, tragic past. Good grief. You ought to be grateful! You got to come to America!"

Sundara took a sharp breath. "You think everybody in the world just sitting there wishing they can leave their homeland for your country?"

"Well, yeah, I think they probably are, if they're smart enough to want a better life."

"But who decide what is a better life? You? Maybe I like my life before. If we choose to come, that one thing, but we are *force* to leave."

"Even so, I still think you laid all this stuff on him so he'd feel sorry for you."

"That not true!"

"Well, come on! You don't think he'd feel the same if you were just the girl next door, do you?"

"But—" Sundara had to smile. It was so obvious. "If I am the girl next door, I am not Sundara Sovann. I am not the girl he like. Cannot separate someone from their past. I am everything I already live through. Just as you are."

Cathy's face was pink up to her eyelids. Her voice broke. "Well, what am I supposed to do? Hope for something awful to happen to me so I can act real brave about it? Then maybe I could compete?"

Sundara sighed. Now she no longer feared Cathy. Now she could tell her off.

And now that she could, she no longer wanted to.

"I'm sorry you unhappy," she said. "I never mean to make everybody so sad." And then she walked on, pretending not to see the clusters of people who'd been lingering, trying to hear.

By the time she reached American lit, the teacher had a note for her. She was to report to Coach Hackenbruck. About Jonathan, of course, but what could the coach want with her?

When she appeared at his door, Coach Hackenbruck swung his feet off his desk and wasted no time on pleasantries. "I don't suppose I have to tell you about McKinnon quitting."

"I just now hear it."

"Well, what do you think we ought to do?"

Sundara blinked at him. "I'm beg your pardon?"

"Look, let's be frank. I know something's going on between you two, and I have a hunch you have something to do with this."

"I never tell him to quit. People blaming me, but this not my idea at all."

"Oh, no? Then tell me why he was in here not forty-five minutes ago raving about the U.S. bombing of Vietnam."

"You mean Cambodia?"

"Whatever. What the hell has it got to do with football?"

"He just upset about that." Sundara's jaw was working. "Maybe he doesn't think football so important compare to the big thing he worry about."

One of the younger assistant coaches came in. Hackenbruck rolled his eyes at him and shook his head.

"McKinnon?" the younger man said.

Hackenbruck nodded.

The assistant coach threw a leg over a chair, sitting in it backward.

They stared at her, waiting.

"I'm telling the true," she said. "Jonatan make up his own mind about this."

"Yeah?" Hackenbruck said. "Well, I'm not so sure he's functioning with all his screws tight these days. If he's got some problems, we'd like to help him. What is it, drugs? Problems at home? Has he given you any other reasons for doing this? I'd blame the whole thing on his concussion except I've smelled this coming on."

Sundara focused on the big bulletin board of newspaper clippings, recognizing some of the pictures from Jonathan's scrapbook. She was trying to remember all the things he'd said about football.

"Well, one thing, he doesn't want to hurt his knee."

"Hurt his knees!" Hackenbruck made a pained face. "What kind of talk is that?"

Sundara tossed her hair back. "Maybe that *smart* talk. Why he want to break his good body for a game he doesn't like?"

"Doesn't like?" the assistant said. "But he's a very talented player."

"Maybe, but that make no matter. He not happy about it."

"Not happy about it." Hackenbruck loaded each word

with disgust. He swiveled to his assistant. "Do you believe this? Kid's our best shot at the state title next year and *he's not happy about it.*" He rested his elbows on his knees and twirled his whistle cord around his finger.

He took a deep breath. "I may look like an old fogy to you," he said to Sundara, "but I'm not so old I don't remember what it feels like to be a seventeen-year-old boy. Now, I know we can't keep them away from you girls, but sometimes you have too much influence on them. And I don't mind telling you, when that's the case, it's a heck of a lot easier on everybody if the girl is somebody who's—well, somebody who—"

"Somebody with white skin?" Sundara said. "Somebody who can do embarrassing dancing on the rally squad? Somebody who think a player who make a touchdown is a big man?"

"Now, don't get upset," the younger coach said, but it was Hackenbruck he glanced at. Fleetingly, Sundara remembered what Kelly had said: Nobody argued with Hackenbruck.

The assistant coach turned back to Sundara. "You've got to give us a break here. We're trying to work this out. And this *is* kind of a tough case."

"Yes, very sad for you. Your star player doesn't like to smash into other people for fun."

Hackenbruck stood up. "Now listen here, young lady—"

"Hold on, Jack. It wasn't her idea, remember? Maybe she'd just as soon have a boyfriend who *is* on the team." He rested his forearms on the back of the chair and smiled at Sundara. "Maybe she could . . . ahh . . . persuade him?" Then he winked.

It was not a nice wink. It was a wink that made her mad.

"No," she said. "No, I can't. Please excuse me. I'm missing my class."

She turned and marched out of their office.

Jonathan caught up with her just before international relations.

"I've been looking for you all over," he said, almost panting. His hair was messier than usual, his flannel shirt hung open over his T-shirt.

"Are you all right?" she asked him. "Everybody talking like you going crazy."

"I'm not going crazy. I'm getting sane."

"But you quit the team?"

"Yeah, right. So what? One more game the doctor didn't want me in anyway."

"But next year . . . ?"

"To hell with next year. Listen, I've got to tell you something." He steered her around the corner where there weren't so many people. "Last night I had this huge fight with my parents."

"They mad about you quit the team?"

"No, no, it's— See, this guy in our church decided to organize a group of doctors to volunteer for the refugee camps. He came over last night and asked my dad if he'd go. I thought, wow, this is great. No waiting around for the government. Just get some doctors together and go. And then—I couldn't believe it when my dad was so waffly. And my mom—for weeks she's been sniffling over all these pictures in the magazines, going, 'Oh, I wish we

LINDA CREW

could *do* something.' Now all of a sudden it's 'Oh, better
not. What if you get a disease? What if you get shot?' "

She stared at him. He was talking so fast. Had he forgotten about the hospital? About telling her he loved her?
First she'd been wondering what they could possibly say
to each other after that. *Then* she'd been expecting to hear
about football. The last thing on her mind was the refugee
camps.

"So of course she runs for her checkbook," he went on,
"like she can send a donation instead of my dad. God, is
that typical?"

"Jonatan, can you calm down? I have a hard time to
understand. They ask your father to help and he doesn't
want to go?"

"Well, he says he hasn't made up his mind, but I don't
believe him. He's backpedaling so fast, coming up with all
this garbage about how it's no use sending doctors if all
they really need is people with shovels to bury the dead.
Keeps saying he's not convinced they've got a workable
system set up for medical people." Jonathan snorted. "Just
making excuses." He raised his eyebrows with a shrug.
"And that's what I told him."

"Jonatan! You say that to your father?"

"Yeah, I did. And I told him I was having a hard time
believing his old stories about the free clinic, working
with poor people and stuff. Not that I think he's lying.
Just that it's hard to imagine he and Mom used to be that
way. Now they seem to think it's enough to sit in their
armchairs and watch it on TV as long as they keep saying
how awful it all is."

"I think you too hard on them."

"That's another thing." Now he actually sounded angry. "I also told him he doesn't deserve the way you look up to him like he's some kind of hero."

"You *are* going crazy, talk back to him like that. You don't understand. When we first come . . . when you having a really bad time, somebody who nice seem like a hero enough."

"Okay, so he was nice. Big deal, Sundara. Basically, he only did what any doctor would do. Prescribing antibiotics isn't heroic."

Sundara looked away from him, down the hall. Why did they have to argue about this? Everyone else was mad at her; she'd been counting on Jonathan to talk about loving her. A girl she didn't even know gave her a dirty look in passing—this silly football thing. And couldn't they just forget Cambodia for once?

"Come on, Sundara, you've seen it on the news. It's going to take a lot more than *nice* to clean up the mess at those refugee camps."

She leveled a look at him. "Don't you talk to me that way."

He took a step back. "Hey, I didn't—"

"Not my fault you mad at your father, not my fault you quit the team." She flashed her eyes at him. "And especially not my fault everybody die in Cambodia!"

CHAPTER 17

Sundara flipped off the kitchen faucet. "Ravy, could you help me, please?"

No answer. Not surprising, with that awful TV noise. She marched past the boys and turned down the volume. If Soka was so concerned about evil American influences, why didn't she ban these shows? Look at little Pon, sitting there big-eyed, learning to believe that a car can squeal tires, fly through the air, and explode in a fireball without the driver even getting scratched.

"Hey, watch out!" Ravy motioned her aside. "You're in our way."

"Could you put the clothes in the dryer, please? And start a load of towels?"

He frowned, intent on the screen. "That's not a boy's job."

Something snapped. "Not a boy's job!" She stepped between him and the chasing cars, hands on her hips. "Would you rather clean up the kitchen? I can't do everything myself, you know. I'm not your servant."

Startled, Ravy rose and went to the garage, eyeing her over his shoulder. Pon looked surprised too.

Well, let them be shocked. She went back to loading the dishwasher. Ravy took to American ways easily enough when they suited him; maybe he'd have to accept a few he didn't like so much. In America it might not be so easy finding the kind of woman who would spoil him. Besides, he knew how to work; it wouldn't hurt him to help out on Saturday. They had so much to catch up on. She hadn't realized how many chores her aunt usually took care of until she stopped.

"Hey, are you all right?" Ravy said now, coming back into the kitchen.

She heard the washer and dryer humming. She sighed. He wasn't a bad boy. He couldn't help it if Soka let him think women would always wait on him.

"Sorry I'm so cross, Ravy. It's been a hard week."

School had been bad enough with all the trouble over Jonathan, and then she dreaded coming home too. After last week's grim news, Soka had grieved herself into a bad cold. She called in sick at work, gave up cooking and cleaning. Every afternoon she waited for Sundara to come home, eager for fresh ears to hear her sorrowing. She hardly ate anything, and managed to kill everyone else's appetite, too, going on at each meal about how terrible it made her feel to eat, knowing so many were starving. "I'm starting to fear we'll never see any of our relatives again in this life," she took to saying, and each time she repeated her dark premonition, the knot in Sundara's stomach clenched tighter.

"Think I'll head over to Kevin's," Ravy said now.

Sundara nodded, envying him. He wanted to leave before Soka, Naro, and Grandmother came back from the grocery store.

She fastened the chain behind him. Well, she'd have her own brief escape when Soka came home, even if it was just a trip to the garbage dump. At least it would give her a chance to see Moni. That was something. Maybe things would have been easier lately if she'd been able to talk with her, let Moni find the black humor in all this. If there was any. Sundara longed to be distracted with talk of married life, but Moni and Chan Seng were busy, she knew, moving into their new apartment. Today, though, she had promised to haul a broken chair away for them.

She whirled through the kitchen, wiping the counters, the stove, getting down on her hands and knees to scrub the floor. Soka must be given no excuse to criticize.

When the kitchen was done, she hurried out to the garage and pulled the dry clothes into a basket. It was cold in the garage now; they'd had to move her cot into the family room, which she disliked. She did not miss the smell of gasoline, but apparently she had developed an American taste for privacy. All week she hardly slept for listening to her aunt roaming the house at night like a restless ghost, sobbing out her regrets, berating herself for the way she'd treated those they'd left behind.

Sundara was in the bedroom folding clothes when she heard them ringing insistently for her to unfasten the door chain. She hurried down the hall with the empty plastic laundry basket.

When she opened the door, the silence was as cold as the rush of foggy air. Grandmother tottered past her to the bedroom, staring straight ahead. Had the clerks been rude to her again? Naro seemed agitated, setting down his sacks, unwinding the scarf from his neck.

Soka dropped her sack of groceries on the counter with an angry *thunk*. "So." She stared at Sundara through narrowed eyes that skewered her like hot pokers. "Why do you *do* these things, Niece? Don't we have troubles enough?"

Sundara glanced at Naro, but he was putting vegetables in the refrigerator, his back squarely turned.

"What have I done?" Sundara's voice was faint.

"What, she asks. *What?* Shamed us all, that's what! We met with the wife of Pok Sary in the produce section, and listen to this: She could not *wait* to tell us that her son saw you and that American boy walking away from the school together."

The laundry basket slipped from Sundara's hand. She reached for the counter to steady herself. "Please let me explain, Younger Aunt."

"Then it's true! Oh, what Fate! Fool that I am, I still held out hope that she lied. What is the matter with you, girl? Sometimes I wonder what life you came from before this. You made a promise to me!"

"But Younger Aunt, I've kept that promise. It's not the way Pok Simo makes it sound. I was upset. Jonatan only wanted to help me. It was the day after we learned the news of Theary and my friend Chamroeun."

Soka paused. That had been a dark day for the whole family; Sundara was safe in pleading grief.

"I wasn't even thinking clearly," Sundara added.

Soka seemed to consider this. "So this is the one and only time since your promise you have talked to this boy?"

Sundara hesitated, remembering the hospital visit.

"Ah-*ha!* So it isn't!" Soka said, pouncing in.

"But you don't understand, Younger Aunt—"

"I understand." Soka's voice gathered intensity. "I understand that you play me like a fool with your deceit. I understand that I am weary of feeding and sheltering a girl who makes me lose face with people like the wife of Pok Sary."

"Now, Soka," Naro said. "Why don't we just forget what that family thinks of us? We have no need to impress them."

"Ha! You're trying to tell me you felt no shame when she practically came out and called our niece a filthy—"

"Soka! Enough!"

Rebuked, Soka turned on Sundara a look of purest loathing. "I wish you would go," she said evenly. "Get out of my sight."

Sundara stepped back as if slapped, then turned and fled the kitchen. Soka moved to follow and finish the tongue-lashing, but Naro blocked her way.

"Little Sister, this is no way to talk!"

"Oh, isn't it? Why do you defend her? She lied to us!"

From the dining area Pon began to cry.

Sundara cringed in the hallway, her heart pounding painfully. All this shouting, and because of her.

Soka's voice rose. "Maybe you'd be more concerned about her if she were the daughter of *your* sister! *Your* responsibility!"

"Responsibility! For four years I've heard nothing but *responsibility* when it comes to our niece. Is that all you think of her? A child needs affection too. You're too hard on her. You've given her all the discipline and none of the love. I hardly think that's what your sister had in mind when she entrusted her to you."

"She didn't want her to turn into a bad girl either."

"She's not a bad girl."

"She's becoming one. Can't you see that?"

Stop! Sundara clapped her hands over her ears. *Please stop!*

"No, I don't see that. I see a girl who's doing her best and having a hard time just like the rest of us. You're not the only one who was uprooted, you know!" Such hot retorts, accusations obviously long held inside, silently rehearsed. Sundara burned.

"And as for these complaints about feeding her," Naro went on, "are you forgetting how hard she worked this summer? She earned a lot of money. And it's not as if she's come home pregnant. But the way you rave on . . . Don't we have enough troubles right now without you worrying about what might or might not happen in the future?"

"But *you* are the one who says we must look to the future, plan for her to be a doctor."

"Yes, that's right. And the girl brings home straight A's. What more do you want?"

"Straight A's won't save her if she's ruined by an American boy. You just want to shut your eyes to the problem because you know this would never have happened if we hadn't come to America!"

"Soka!" There was a shocked pause. "Now I know for certain you're out of your mind. We would all be *dead* if we hadn't come to America. And you know it."

This was unreal, a bad dream. People did not shout this way, rage at each other . . .

Sundara's uncle was at her side, a pulse pounding in

his temple, surprise at his own anger plain on his face. He put his hand on her shoulder, thinking. He glanced back toward the kitchen.

"It might be best if you went ahead to the dump. We must all regain our senses."

Sundara nodded numbly. But where could she go if Soka decided to throw her out for good? To a city to beg on the streets as she'd heard some runaways did? A government orphan home, living with strangers . . . ?

Naro put the car keys in her hand. "I don't think Soka even knows what she's saying anymore."

She knows, Sundara thought. Soka had said nothing Sundara hadn't already known she'd felt, nothing she hadn't heard in her voice many times before.

"I will speak to her while you're gone."

Sundara pulled her rubber mud boots from the hall closet and jammed her feet into them. "Please don't trouble yourself, Uncle." Couldn't he see? It didn't matter what anyone said. Soka would always hate her. She hadn't been able to save Soka's baby, and Soka was never going to forgive her. Sundara opened the front door to the fog. The very air in this house was poisoned with Soka's hatred; she couldn't stand to breathe it another minute.

She longed to spill this to Moni, but when her friend opened her apartment door, the words wouldn't come. Sundara leaned against the doorjamb, still weak with the force of Soka's anger.

"Sundara! What is it? Are you sick? Oh, of course, your friend Chamroeun. I was so sorry to hear that news."

Sundara shook her head.

"The American boy, then?"

"Yes, no. Oh Moni, it's everything. My chest feels tight enough to break open. This time Soka will throw me out, I'm sure of it."

"Oh, I can't believe that. Come in now. Sit down."

"No, no, I must go to the dump."

"Just a minute, then." Moni went in and spoke with her husband. "I'd better come with you, Little Sister. We can talk in the car."

But Sundara couldn't talk, couldn't explain. She was weary of trying. Chamroeun was dead, Soka would always hate her, they would never see their family again. She could never fit in with the Americans, yet now that she'd known Jonathan, she could never accept an arranged marriage to a stranger. What was the point? What was the point of trying anymore? What was the point of anything?

At the deserted dump, Sundara drove the station wagon up the muddy road to the top and backed it to the edge of the steep slope. She opened the door. The stench of rotting garbage hit her in the face, turned her stomach. She put on her work gloves as Moni got out the other side. Then they opened the back hatch and Moni pulled out her chair. Taking short, quick breaths of the stinking fog, Sundara opened the plastic cans and spilled the contents of each down the slope. She shoved the cans back in, slammed the door, stripped off the gloves.

Then she saw it. Down in the rubble, a tiny arm reached through the garbage toward her. She shut her eyes, heart pounding.

"Little Sister, what is it?"

Cautiously, Sundara opened her eyes. Still there. She stared, trembling.

Moni squinted in the same direction. "Oh, it's just a doll." She smiled tentatively. "A broken doll?"

Sundara fought for breath, stumbling back against the car, pressing her head between her hands. "The baby . . . Oh, the baby . . ."

"Sundara, what are you talking about?" Moni peered down into the rubble again. "It's not a baby. It's a doll. Can't you see that?"

"No, no . . ." Sundara knew a doll from a baby, and she knew an omen when she saw one too. She sank to the mud.

"Sundara!" Moni tried to pull her up but she fell back against the tire.

"No use, Moni. No use." She was sobbing now, powerless to stop it from engulfing her . . . the brief instant of hope at the baby's stirring, the bewilderment at pulling back the *krama*, and—*God in heaven*—the last shudder of life, the tiny hand slowly uncurling its fingers. . . . Seeing it all again now, her cry rose. "*Nooooo!*"

Moni fell back, hand to her mouth.

"Nooo! She'll be with me forever!" Sundara cried.

"*Please,*" Moni begged. "What are you talking about?"

"Soka's baby! Oiee! I might as well have her lashed in my *krama* for the rest of my life."

"What is this? Soka had a baby?"

Sundara nodded crazily, holding her head as if to crush it. "And I let her die! I was supposed to take care of her and instead I let her die!"

"Oh . . . oh, merciful God . . ." Moni glanced around, wringing her hands. "I've got to get you home."

"I have no home!"

"Sundara, you've got to get up. I can't drive your uncle's car. I only have my learner's permit!"

This struck Sundara as wildly, absurdly funny. She began laughing hysterically. Moni, who knew how to keep babies alive, who had tramped hundreds of miles through the jungle alone, afraid to drive a car!

But Moni's voice sounded wavery and close to tears. "Don't laugh like that, Little Sister! You're scaring me!"

Sundara went back to crying. "Just leave me here, Moni. Just leave me."

Suddenly, Moni's strong arms were around her, dragging her to the car, wrestling her inside.

Moni got in the driver's side, put her hands on the wheel, and drew a deep breath. "Heaven protect us," she said. She turned on the ignition.

Sundara sobbed all the way home. Her hair stuck to her wet face as she huddled on the front seat, a muddy heap. Finally, the car stopped. The door on her side opened and hands reached for her, arms lifted her out. Moni had summoned Naro. Supporting Sundara between them, they half carried her to the house.

"One look at this broken doll," Moni said, "and she fell down in a fit."

"She was upset when she left. She and Soka, you know . . ."

"Yes, I could see that, but what is this business of Soka's baby?"

"Ah, she spoke of that?"

Soka came in from the living room, trailed by Grandmother. "What's the matter with her?"

"She's gone crazy," Moni said. "It's about your baby, Soka."

"My baby? My baby daughter?"

"Niece, please calm yourself," Naro said. "It's not so bad as all this."

"I'm sorry, I'm sorry," Sundara cried. "Younger Aunt, I'm so sorry!"

"Now, now . . ." They led her to her cot in the family room, where she collapsed in a fresh outpouring of tears.

"Why can't she stop crying?" Naro said, a hint of panic in his voice.

"Because it's not in her power to do so," was Grandmother's reply, strong and surprisingly full of authority. "Can you not see what is before your eyes?"

Vaguely, Sundara was aware of them staring at her. What was it Grandmother could see that they could not?

"The spirit of Soka's baby," Grandmother announced, "has taken over Sundara's body."

A fearful silence, then the sound of someone else's crying mingled with Sundara's.

"Why is mother crying?" Pon piped up. "What's the matter with Sundara?"

"Son," Grandmother said, "why not take this little one back into the bedroom. He's had enough upset for one day. The spirit will only frighten him. Let us women deal with it."

The drapes were hastily drawn and in a moment, Sundara smelled burning incense. Grandmother perched on the edged of the cot.

"Little Spirit," she said, rubbing Sundara's back. "Do not punish our girl this way. Please fly away from her body."

Sundara kept crying. Was she crazy? Had the spirit of Soka's baby truly seized her? She heard their soft, chorused pleadings at a distance, as if she were underwater and the three women crooning to the spirit were above. She was swimming, drowning in her own tears, beyond caring, crying for every sad thing she had never cried about before.

"Oieee! Grandmother! Naro was right. I have been too hard on her, poor girl."

Was it possible? Was that really Soka, coming to sit on the side of the cot, stroking her hair? Sundara didn't dare raise her head, as if to look at them would dispel their concern, break the aura as they took turns pleading with the baby's spirit.

Tears soaked her bedding and still more welled up. She cried for the baby. She cried for Chamroeun. She cried for the rest of her family and the thoughtless things she'd said to them, the loving things she'd left unsaid. She cried for the foolishness of having argued with her mother over a parasol, not knowing the last chance for *I love you* was slipping away. And, as long as it was pouring out like an endless torrent, she cried for Jonathan. All this to the soothing, continuous murmurings of the women.

After a long time, Sundara's weeping finally ceased, and she lay exhausted, not sleeping but not moving either. She heard a deep sigh.

"Grandmother, you must rest," Soka said. "We will stay with her."

"She's all right, then?" Naro asked quietly from the door.

"The spirit has flown," Grandmother said. The cot creaked as she pushed herself up, letting Moni take her place.

Sundara lay there listening as Soka and Moni spoke in low tones. They seemed to think she was completely unconscious.

"It's true." Soka sniffed. "I haven't been fair to her."

"She thinks you hate her," Moni said bluntly.

"Ah! Don't tell me that!" Soka wept.

"How *do* you feel about her, then? Do you *like* your niece?"

A pause. "I . . . I don't know. Terrible, isn't it? I guess it is as Naro said. I've thought of her as a responsibility, that's all."

"But she's such a sweet girl. And so smart."

"Yes. She is smart. She knows so much more than I about so many things. But is that right? I'm older. I'm supposed to guide her, but how can I?"

Moni sighed. "Maybe the old patterns won't always work anymore."

"Every time I look at her I . . . I see her mother. I worry that I'm not raising her right. You have eyes. You can see she is too pretty for her own good. If she loves a boy and something bad happens . . . Oiee! I could never forgive myself!"

"I wonder why we find it so much harder to forgive ourselves than to forgive others. You can't protect her from everything."

"But she *is* my responsibility, even if Naro is mad at me for always saying that. I want to see her happily married, like you, to a good Khmer."

"Well, maybe she will be someday, who can say? But in the meantime, why let yourself be eaten up by worry and guilt? Look at us. All of us. I'm tired of our guilt."

There was a long moment of quiet, then Soka spoke. "She really thinks that was her fault? About the baby?"

"Apparently so. And imagine my surprise. Neither of you ever even mentioned this baby."

"Ah, well. I guess I've tried to pretend it never happened." She sniffed, fighting back tears again. "You have to understand, Moni. I was crazy sick and out of my mind on the ship. I remember opening my eyes and seeing her sitting there, trying to make the baby drink something. *The baby's going to die*, I remember thinking, and it was odd, feeling so calm about it. But you see, I thought I was going to die too. I thought we would all die. When I came to my senses and the baby . . . the baby wasn't there anymore, I thought, oh, God, why did I let myself get sick? That was my baby! I should have got up, I should have done something . . ."

Finally, Soka broke down and cried. She cried long and hard.

Sundara dozed off to the sound of her sobbing.

When she awoke later, the scent of incense was gone, replaced by the garlicky aroma of dinner cooking. Someone had pulled off her boots, but the rest of her clothes felt clammy. She changed into dry jeans and shirt, combed her hair. She was hungry.

When she appeared in the doorway, all eyes turned her way. She lowered her lids, embarrassed.

Soka guided her to a chair and put a bowl of sour beef soup before her. "How are you feeling?" she said with unusual solicitude. "I don't suppose you remember anything?"

Sundara looked down, her face warm.

"You see," Grandmother said to the others, "it is as I told you. When this happens they never do."

But Sundara did. She had heard Soka's private thoughts. She felt shy now, trying to pretend she did not remember Soka's arms around her.

She spoke with downcast eyes. "You are right, Grandmother. I remember nothing."

CHAPTER 18

"What a surprising thing," Naro said, coming into the bedroom where Soka and Sundara were changing sheets together. "Can you imagine who was just on the phone? That Dr. McKinnon. And listen to this: He wants our niece to teach him Khmer."

Sundara lowered her pillow with the case only half on. "Why?" Soka demanded.

"He's volunteered for the refugee camps in Thailand and he needs to be able to speak with the people." He gave Soka a pointed look. "There now, aren't you ashamed to be looking so suspicious?"

"Well," she said, somewhat humbled. "He *is* a good

man, isn't he?" She avoided Sundara's eyes. "But why our niece?"

"Ah, well, he tells me she would be a good teacher because she speaks English so well, yet still remembers her native tongue."

Soka's brows went together. "What shall we do? Shall we allow this?"

"Shall we *allow* this? Why Soka, naturally I've already told him we're honored he's chosen her."

Sundara shook the pillow into the case.

"But what about the son? Maybe this is simply a trick for them to be together."

"A fancy trick indeed. Would a man journey to the other side of the world just for a trick? Little Sister, if a man is willing to help our people like this, I am certainly not going to insult him by forbidding my niece to teach him Khmer just because his son is smart enough to know a pretty girl when he sees one!"

"Yes, I suppose that would be rude," Soka conceded, her voice small. Then, as if her approval were still needed, as if Naro hadn't already given his consent, she turned to Sundara. "Very well, but you must spend every moment teaching him Khmer. No wasting time with his son." Plainly, Soka meant what she said, but it seemed to Sundara her voice lacked its old edge.

"Yes, Younger Aunt."

"Imagine," Soka said, "a wealthy man like him going to the refugee camps. I have to admit, sometimes the Americans surprise me. Our upper-class Khmer people wouldn't *dream* of lowering themselves like that. But then, from the first time we met him, I knew this Dr. McKinnon was a good man, the sort who sees not only with his eyes. Haven't I always said that?"

Sundara and Naro exchanged glances, suppressing smiles.

"Yes, Younger Aunt."

"Another thing," Sundara told Dr. McKinnon. "You must never step over somebody who lie down on a mat. You do that, it kind of like shoveling dirt on them."

"Good thing that doesn't bother me," Jonathan said from the open French doors separating his father's home office from the living room. His back rested on the doorjamb, his worn-out running shoes were braced against the opposite side. Whenever Sundara came to tutor, he made this his spot, and his parents had to step over him every time they passed.

"But you sitting there not the same thing." Sundara gave him an arch look. "You are the son. To show respect, you should stand."

"Oh." He grinned sheepishly, sliding up, dropping his feet to the carpet.

"You could learn a lot here," his father said. He turned back to his notebook. "Do not step over people."

Sundara smiled at Jonathan. She didn't care how he sat or stood in his father's office, as long as he was there, watching her, making her feel warm and loved every evening.

Besides teaching Dr. McKinnon useful Khmer phrases —Do you vomit? Do you bleed? Are your parents alive?— Sundara was also explaining Khmer customs. She told him about not touching the children's heads. She warned him not to be surprised at how the men stand close to talk, how they hug and hold hands with each other. "Not like here," she told him. "There, nobody think anything about it."

She described the practice of *kaob*—how they rub the edge of a coin on someone, hard, for healing. Sometimes American doctors didn't understand. They saw the bruises and accused the Khmers of beating their children.

Mrs. McKinnon would pop in on their tutoring sessions when she came home from her own meetings, filling her husband in on things she'd found out while he was at work—immunizations he'd need, passport details. According to Jonathan, once his father had made up his mind to go, she had stopped raising objections. How could she argue when it was so clearly the right thing to do? The sort of thing they'd dreamed of doing when they were younger? Maybe they *had* gotten too comfortable these last few years. . . .

But in spite of Mrs. McKinnon's efforts at being cheerful and supportive, Sundara detected a certain desperation in the way she kept bringing in heavily laden snack trays, as if she feared her husband wouldn't get food at all once he left. And concern crept into her voice when she talked on the phone. "Just how easy is it to get malaria?" Sundara overheard her say one time, and, "Well of *course* I'm worried. What do you think? I heard on NPR today they're still shelling around one of the camps. . . ."

On the Saturday before Thanksgiving, Sundara went with Soka to visit a new Khmer family. An awkward business—lugging the cardboard boxes of church-donated clothes up to their second-floor apartment while wearing sarongs. Soka had insisted they wear them, thinking this familiar touch might be comforting to the newcomers.

Gratefully, Sundara set down her boxes at number twenty-seven as Soka pushed the bell. When the door opened, Sundara and Soka glanced at each other in surprise.

The wife of Pok Sary!

"What are you two doing here?" The woman stared at Sundara. *You are the girl who goes with Americans,* her sneer said, making Sundara want to shrivel with shame.

But Soka drew herself up tall. "The church people have sent us to show the new lady how to turn on her stove and work the faucets."

The wife of Pok Sary blocked the door. "Perhaps they didn't realize," she said in her shrill voice, "that the new lady is the widow of a very high-ranking military officer. It would hardly be appropriate for you to be telling her how to do things, would it?"

Sundara held her breath.

"Pardon me," Soka said, "but I don't think whose husband was what in the old Kampuchea is nearly so important as who knows best how to get along in America now."

How proud Sundara felt to hear Soka speak up this way!

But the wife of Pok Sary was not enjoying it at all. "I know perfectly well how to operate the appliances," she said.

"I'm sure you do," Soka replied, never relaxing her hard smile. "I think it's nice that you've decided to be neighborly. But as long as my niece and I are here, we'd like to deliver these clothes and pay our respects." She nodded at Sundara. "Come, Niece."

The wife of Pok Sary took a step back in surprise as Soka marched in and found the new family. Taking a cue from her aunt, Sundara put her palms together and bowed to the new woman, not a low bow, but a friendly one, between equals.

"We wish to welcome you to Willamette Grove," Soka said formally, but with warmth. "If there is any way we can help you, please honor my family by calling on us." Head high, she gave the wife of Pok Sary a slight nod as they went out the door.

"I'm sick of the way she treats us," Soka began raging to Naro the moment she and Sundara got home. "She might as well come out and call us dirty peasants! How long do they think they can hang on to the past? We've made a place for ourselves here, worked without sparing our hands. They think it's so wonderful to be born high-class, but I think it means more when you've had to work your way up. Oiee! When I think of those hard times when you had to ride a bicycle home from work in the freezing rain, how you'd fall down on the living room carpet and lie like a frozen corpse. Every night I thought, this is the end, he will break, he will never get up. But the next day you always went off to wash dishes again. Day after day after day."

"Come now, Little Sister, that is past. We survived."

"Yes, but it wasn't easy. And if they think we should just forget how hard we've worked for our house and jobs, just act like we're nothing and bow down to them . . ."

"Now don't upset yourself."

"I'm only taking your advice, Naro. I've thought about what you said the other day and you're right. What do I care what they think? *We* are the ones who have been here almost the required five years." She turned to Sundara. "Do you know what that means, Niece? We will become

American citizens, and American citizens don't have to make themselves low to anybody! Why, we could even go rescue our relatives in Kampuchea and nobody would dare touch us! Not when we told them we are citizens of the United States of America!"

This tirade bewildered Sundara. Sometimes it seemed Soka couldn't decide whether being American was the best thing in the world or the worst.

She headed for the garage to change her sarong for jeans. Maybe their mistake was in feeling they had to choose, fearing they couldn't be American without giving up being Khmer. Why couldn't they be both? In the end, after all, what was more American than coming from someplace else, bringing another culture with you? As she stepped around the corner, she heard Soka's voice drop.

"And I'm especially tired of the way she needles me about our niece," Soka said. "Even when it's just with her eyes. If her son is so smart, so much better, why are no doctors asking *him* to teach them Khmer?"

Sundara pulled a pumpkin pie from the oven. Although she didn't much care for the taste, she'd learned the traditional recipe. It was important to celebrate these American holidays properly.

But somehow Thanksgiving always made her feel more sad than thankful. It reminded her of the Khmer celebration of plenty, the Water Festival. Even though the pageants had ended with the war, she still remembered the lighted floats on the river, could almost feel her mother's hand around hers as they joined the throng watching the colorful procession from the banks. The American Pilgrims were thankful for wild turkeys and Indian corn. But what about the Mekong? What about the Mother of Waters? A river that annually flooded their rice paddies with fertility. A river so bountiful with fish that when the monsoons were over and the Tonle Sap began to drain, the people had only to walk out and fill their baskets with the fish that flopped in the puddles! Surely America was an amazing country, and worth feeling thankful for. But the way some Americans talked, you'd think this was the *only* country on earth worth loving.

From the doorway she glanced around the crowded living room, disappointed not to find Moni and Chan Seng among those gathered on the spread-out mats.

"You invited them, didn't you?" she asked Soka.

Soka basted the turkey. "Of course, but I think—ah, she's not well." Was Soka avoiding more questions or just preoccupied? Even if this did mark her third American-style turkey, preparing it still took concentration.

The feast was lively. Everyone wanted to know more about this Dr. McKinnon who was going to the camps. Was Soka's niece really teaching him Khmer? Had Naro and Soka seen the inside of his house? The Cambodians pored over the beautiful book he had given Sundara, a colored pictorial of Angkor Wat. And the letters! Everyone had something for the doctor to post on the camp bulletin board.

"Look at this," Soka said to Sundara, pulling her aside at one point, producing a fat envelope with obvious satisfaction. "A letter from Pok Sary and his wife for the camps. They humbled themselves to have Prom Kea pass it to us."

For once Sundara's family and friends had more than bad news and frightening rumors to trade. Although it was terrible to watch the suffering on the television, per-

LINDA CREW

haps some good could come from it. The Americans were
finally being forced to pay attention to the desperate situation in Kampuchea; maybe they could help. Everyone
wanted to talk about that.

After dinner, while they were eating and politely
praising Sundara's pies, the phone rang. A moment later a
joyful shriek split the hum of conversation, and Soka
rushed from the kitchen in streaming tears.

"It's my sister Valinn!" she cried. "She's coming to
America!"

"You know how Grandmother always says we must do
good deeds," Soka said, "so our next life will be better?"

"Yes, Younger Aunt." The guests had gone now. Sundara and Soka were alone in the kitchen, cleaning up.

"Well, Grandmother might frown to hear me say this,
but I am beginning to think we don't have to wait until
our next life for our reward. I'm getting a reward in this
life, aren't I, with Valinn coming?"

"Yes, it seems so, and surely you deserve it, Younger
Aunt. You have helped so many people."

"That's true, I have," she said matter-of-factly, "but I
don't think that's why God is rewarding me now."

Sundara waited. She wished Soka would speak plainly.
Obviously her aunt had changed since that terrible day
when Sundara's pent-up feelings had burst out. But was it
because of that? Or was it her change in attitude toward
the family of Pok Simo? Or even her new respect for the
McKinnons?

But Soka only wished to go over the details about
Valinn again, to revel in her happiness, her hope that this
might signal the start of good fortune for their family.

Sundara murmured responses, sorry and a little ashamed she did not feel more excited.

"You are wishing it could be your mother, aren't you?"

Sundara glanced at Soka, startled. Were her guilty thoughts so plain to see, then? She slid a dry plate onto the stack in the cupboard. Good news was good news; one shouldn't complain. Still, another aunt was not the same as a father or mother, brother or sister.

"I'm sorry, Younger Aunt. I cannot help it."

"Of course not. I, too, pray for the day when your mother and the rest of your family can come."

Soka's sympathy surprised Sundara.

"I always loved your mother," Soka went on. "If she ever *can* come, I want to be able to say, 'You see, Elder Sister, how I've taken care of your daughter?' I could never forgive myself if she decided she'd made a mistake in sending you to Réam. After all, I promised you'd be safe with me."

"Oh, she didn't care about that."

Soka's brows went together. "Of course she did."

"But Younger Aunt, if she worried for my safety, would she have let me board a plane even as bombs fell on the airport? All she cared about was making sure you had plenty of help."

"And you *were* a good helper. But Little One, you were only thirteen, and I did have a servant girl. Surely you didn't think helping me was your mother's main thought? Why, she was frantic to get you out of Phnom Penh. She would have sent Mayoury, too, except she was too little and the plane tickets were almost impossible to get."

Sundara stopped drying the pan she held.

"Have you never thought of this?" Soka asked gently. "The plane may have been dangerous, but you are alive. If you had stayed in Phnom Penh . . ." She trailed off, shaking her head.

Sundara searched Soka's face, puzzled. She had always felt somehow punished by their decision to send her off. She'd never stopped to think that her ultimate safety had been part of the plan.

"Are you sure of this, Younger Aunt? Because if you could have been there and heard the way she kept after me, making me promise to . . ."

Soka waited. "Yes, go on. Making you promise to what?"

Sundara hesitated, then looked Soka in the eyes. "To take good care of . . . the baby." There. She'd said it. The baby.

"Ahh . . ."

"And Younger Aunt? I tried. I—I did the best I could."

"I know you did." Soka took the pan from Sundara's hands and put it in the cupboard. "Sundara, you were nothing but a child yourself. This is what I've been wanting to tell you. . . . Until that day when her little spirit . . . Well, I had no *idea* you thought . . . If anything, you see, it was *my* fault. She was my baby. On the ship . . . I should have got up. I should have—"

"No, Younger Aunt, you couldn't have. Not sick the way you were. No one could."

"You don't think so?"

"Of course not."

Soka sighed. "Well, perhaps you're right. After all, wasn't bad karma certain, leaving our house that way without the ceremonies?"

"I suppose," Sundara said, but she was not thinking about luck. She was still struggling with guilt, and her voice trembled with the most important question of all. "Then you really don't blame me that the baby died?"

"No! God in heaven, of course it wasn't your fault. Now, never let me hear you say that again! Don't I have enough on my conscience without thinking I made you suffer such guilt all this time?"

Not my fault, Sundara was thinking. *Not my fault*. Her spirit rose.

"So your mother made you promise to take care of my baby," Soka said. Sundara nodded. "And she made *me* promise to take care of *you*!" She laughed with a touch of helplessness. "She better get here someday, Niece! I want her to appreciate what a lot of trouble you and I have gone through to keep our promises!"

Sundara could only shake her head at this. They were bound together in the funny, sad joke. Would her mother ever learn how hard they'd tried?

Well, there are always sad thoughts for those who want to be sad, Sundara told herself, but now she had this to hold to: Losing the baby was not her fault. Soka did not blame her. And in spite of the angry last words, her parents had hurried her onto that plane for a reason she'd never let herself believe: love.

The kitchen was warm as she and Soka worked together, the quiet between them easy. What a Thanksgiving this had turned out to be! The clinking of the dishes sounded to Sundara like sweet, peaceful music. Temple bells.

CHAPTER 19

Mrs. McKinnon appeared in the doorway of her husband's office. "Honey," she said to him, "you have *got* to
get some rest." She glanced at her watch. "You're going to
be exhausted tomorrow."

Tomorrow.

Dr. McKinnon looked startled. "So this is really going
to happen." He shrugged at Jonathan and Sundara. "Been
so busy boning up, I guess the reality hasn't had a chance
to sink in."

The medical team was leaving in the morning. The
doctors, nurses, and paramedics from different towns
were to meet in Portland for breakfast near the airport. A
minister would pray with them. The flight went first to

Seattle, then Hong Kong, and, finally, Bangkok. Jonathan's father would be gone for two months. Once he left Bangkok for the camp, he would not even be able to phone home.

Dr. McKinnon took off his reading glasses and rubbed the bridge of his nose. His desk was littered with empty coffee cups and Xerox copies of articles about tropical diseases. A stack of medical books threatened to slide onto the floor.

"Actually, now that it's time," he said, "I can't wait to get going." He pushed back his chair and began putting the tapes of Khmer phrases they'd made in a satchel.

Mrs. McKinnon smiled weakly.

Sundara and Jonathan traded glances. Sundara couldn't blame her for worrying; she worried about Dr. McKinnon too.

"You must take care yourself," she admonished him now. "If the camp in a jungle, watch out for the tiger."

"Richard." Mrs. McKinnon turned pale. "She's kidding, isn't she?"

He laughed shortly. "Tigers'll be the least of our problems. With forty or fifty thousand people crammed in Sakeo, I'm sure the tigers'll smell us and stay away."

"Right." She didn't look reassured. She gave Jonathan a crooked smile. "Going to be a strange Christmas around here, isn't it?"

"We'll save it, Mom. We'll have it when he comes home."

When he comes home. The words hung in the air.

Mrs. McKinnon opened her eyes and blinked hard.

Dr. McKinnon caught this. "Now, Gwen . . ."

She waved him off, shaking her head, collecting herself.

"I'm going to be fine . . ."

She nodded. Then she stopped and took a deep breath.

"Well!" She stuck her hands on her hips, surveying the cluttered office. "At least I'll be glad to get this place cleaned out."

Jonathan and his father looked at each other. No one said anything for a moment.

Sundara took her jacket from the back of her chair. Their time was up. She had helped Dr. McKinnon all she could. She had no excuse to stay any longer tonight. She would have no excuse to come ever again.

She opened her book bag.

"Dr. McKinnon, this for you." She handed him a small wooden plaque that she'd lettered in Khmer script. "You will honor me if you hang this where you work at the camp. I'm thinking some people might be fear of your white face, and you so big, so I make this to help them know you are a good man, one who see not only with his eyes."

He cleared his throat. "Ah . . . thank you. Thank you very much. *You* honor *me.*"

"What does it say?" Mrs. McKinnon asked.

"I try to translate what that man Albert Schweitzer say, the word over the hospital door. 'Here, at whatever hour you come, you will find light and help and human kindness.'" She hesitated. "Someday, Dr. McKinnon, I like very much to follow in your footprint."

Dr. McKinnon placed his huge palms together, dipping his forehead in a Khmer bow of respect.

"Ahh. . . ." she breathed, beaming. "You learn good!"

When all their good-byes were said, Jonathan walked Sundara out to her car. The mist drifted down through the porch light.

"I feel like such a jerk," he said. "All my raving about them never making a commitment. I guess I felt safe, shooting off my mouth—I never really thought he'd *do* it."

She opened the car door. "You sorry you not showing more respect or sorry he going?"

"Both, I guess. I just feel so . . . *responsible*. He wouldn't be doing this if I hadn't freaked out. He said that. Said I forced him to take a closer look at himself. I thought that's what I wanted . . . but now that he's actually going . . . well, I know *somebody's* got to, but . . ." He stopped, studied her face. "This must sound pretty selfish to you. Thousands of people over there—your relatives, maybe—and I'm worried about one guy, just because he happens to be my dad."

"One person matter a lot," she said without looking at him, "when the one person somebody you love."

A long silence.

"Your mother worry about him too."

"Yeah." He leaned on the open car door. "You know, I always thought people who did this sort of thing just went off, all brave and full of conviction. It never occurred to me they might have mixed feelings. Now I see there's a lot more to it. It's not that my dad's so brave, see. Actually he's scared. But he's going anyway. That's what gets me. He's scared but he's psyched up too."

"Your father a special person. Don't I try to tell you this all the time?"

"Yeah, yeah, okay. Call me a slow learner." Jonathan sighed. "I bet none of us'll sleep tonight."

Sundara had the car keys in her hand. There didn't seem to be much else to say.

"Well," he said, "looks like this is it, then."

She nodded.

"I've gotten spoiled, having you over here every night." He kicked at a bit of gravel. Then, as if the wet pavement had given him a brilliant idea, his head snapped up. "What if we told your folks *I* needed lessons in Khmer?"

They laughed, but only briefly.

"Oh, Sundara." He looked like he was in pain, like he wanted to hit something. Suddenly he reached out and took her into his arms.

Surprise stiffened her for a moment, then she sank against him. She let out a long, trembling sigh. Nothing had ever felt so good. She smelled the rain on him, felt his heart pounding under the damp flannel of his shirt.

And then he held her a little away. His hands slid up her cheeks and into her hair and he was pulling her mouth to his.

A kiss, she was thinking. A real kiss. So this is—

It was over too quickly.

"Oh, Jonatan . . ."

He released her. "I know, I know." He backed away, walking a crazed circle. "You don't have to say it. I shouldn't have done that. I'm sorry, okay? I'm really sorry." He stopped, faced her. "But I just couldn't help it."

Sundara bit her lip, still tasting him, her gaze fixed on his chest. "Going to have to last me a long time, thinking about that." She raised her eyes. "Maybe you could do again?"

CHAPTER 20

Sundara steered Pon onto the escalator at the Portland International Airport, banging the bulky gift box against the moving handrail as she stepped on behind him. Readjusting her load at the top, she scanned a video screen listing the flights. Ahead of her, Soka and Naro tried to hurry Grandmother along.

"Younger Aunt! No need to rush. The plane will be forty-five minutes late."

Soka stopped. "Oh, no! I cannot wait that long. Not after all the waiting we have already endured!"

Sundara caught up with the others and together they peered down the long corridor at the lighted signs of the gate numbers, white against blue.

"Gate forty-six," Naro said, checking the note he'd made.

Naturally, Ravy already knew where to go. "It's down at the end."

Sundara coaxed Pon through the metal detector and waited for the box containing Valinn's heavy jacket to be X-rayed and reappear on the conveyor belt. They had not forgotten how cool the climate in Oregon had first seemed to them, even arriving in the summer. How much harder it would be for Valinn, coming at this dreary time of year, December twenty-first, one of the shortest, darkest days. It didn't seem a good omen, but maybe there was comfort in knowing this was the worst; from now on the days would improve in light and length.

Two other Khmer families, friends from Portland, were already sitting in a row of plastic seats, dressed in their best American-style suits and bright dresses. One of the families had known Valinn, and the husband she'd lost, when they all lived in Takeo. Soon more families came, and the children chased each other around the terminal, stopping only to watch the big jets take off or land.

Sundara watched the wind-driven sheets of water ripple across the runway. She was glad Valinn would have family to meet her. Much better than the finish of her own long flight, in darkness, from the Philippines . . .

The harsh light had blinded her when the plane door opened that morning. She remembered squinting at her first dismaying glimpse of America—nothing but gray pavement. Clutching Pon, she had let the surge of weary passengers carry her down the stairs. Now they were in the terminal. She couldn't see over heads. She stood on tiptoes. Wait! Naro and Soka. Where were they? Pon began crying again. Oh no, more diarrhea. Frantic, she threaded her way through the crowd. "Uncle! Younger Aunt!" Lost. Tears welling up. And the shame of it, looking so dirty, knowing she smelled bad . . .

Suddenly she saw her, one of those strange black people, darker than a Khmer. On her collar a little pin, a red cross. Didn't that mean help? Catching her eye, Sundara spoke only with her heart and hoped the meaning showed on her face. *Please help me.* To her utter surprise, the big woman took one look and answered by embracing her, never mind Pon and the diarrhea. She had taken the child from Sundara's arms and soon gathered their family together again. God alone could have sent such a person, Sundara had thought many times since then, a woman ready to open her arms to a stranger. . . .

She turned away from the window now and glanced around the waiting room. Surely it would be less frightening for Valinn, with family here to reassure her, remind her as many times as she needed to hear it that she truly was safe at last. She was in America.

"Moni!" Sundara said, spotting her friend. "How good to see you. We missed you at Thanksgiving."

"Ah, I'm sorry I couldn't be there. But how have you been, Little One? We were so worried about you."

"I'm well, Moni. Things are better." Sundara flushed, remembering the day she cried. She brightened her voice now. "I wasn't expecting so many people. I'm sure most of them don't even know my aunt."

"But she is Khmer, and such a short time ago in our homeland. When Prom Kea's wife offered me a ride today I was so grateful. I have so many things to ask your aunt . . . if she ever saw people I know, that sort of thing."

"Yes, there'll be questions for her from every mouth. Ah, I wish the plane would hurry. Did you hear it's late?"

She glanced at the big clock suspended from the ceiling. "We still have another hour."

"We do? Oh, good. I wanted to buy a rose on the way in, but I didn't think I'd have time. Come walk to the flower cart with me."

Sundara went to tell Soka where she was going and found her aunt feverish with excitement. It was a party, and she was the center of attention, the closest relative to the guest of honor.

"Yes, yes, you can go. But hurry back. Everyone must be here when she steps off the plane!"

Sundara joined Moni. "Soka's almost *too* excited."

"Who can blame her? After so many years, to see her sister again . . ."

Sundara thought of Mayoury with a pang. Had her own mother loved her spoiled baby sister Soka the same way Sundara loved Mayoury?

Moni picked out a pink rose with a bit of baby's breath and fern and paid for it.

"You really don't have to do this," Sundara said.

"Oh, I want to. I'm so honored to share your happy day. I don't want to be empty-handed."

Sundara smiled. "Well, now. I want to hear all about what it's like to be married."

Moni glanced at her. "Soka didn't tell you?"

"Tell me what?"

"About the reason I didn't come to Thanksgiving."

Sundara tilted her head. "She said you were sick."

"Ah. Well, I was sick, in a way. Sick in my spirit."

"Moni, what's the matter?" Now that she thought of it, Moni did not seem her usual lighthearted self.

"Remember the letter you helped me write? Well, I got an answer." She looked up from a fuzzy tiger in the gift

]202[

shop window. "Sundara, my husband has another wife and two children alive in one of the camps."

Sundara stared. "Another wife? How can that be?"

Moni sighed. "I didn't want to worry you about that before. He was so certain they were dead. But they're alive, and they want to come here."

"Oh, Moni." Sundara tried to think what this would mean. She was torn between happiness for the news of life, and sorrow for Moni. "What does Chan Seng say?"

She shrugged. "He wants them to come." She looked down at her rose. "He wants me to divorce him."

"I can't believe that. He seems to love you so much."

"But she is his number one wife. I am only wife number two. Of course, Soka tells me not to divorce him. 'You are his number one wife in America,' she says. A man cannot have two wives here, so unless I agree to a divorce, the Immigration people cannot help him."

"You're not going to agree to it, are you? It doesn't seem fair after all you've been through."

"But he cannot just close his eyes to his first wife, can he? She writes to him that she will wait forever for him to rescue her."

Sundara thought how she would feel, sitting in a refugee camp with her children after a harrowing escape, finding out that her husband had started a new life in America without her, a new life with a new woman. She remembered the song that always brought them to tears.

"I'm giving him a divorce," Moni said. "I don't want to be married to a man when only his body is here and his spirit is somewhere else."

"Oh, Moni. Why didn't Soka tell me?"

"Ah, well, she probably hates to have you see that this is the way it turns out with our people these days. It makes it harder for her to insist you save yourself for a Khmer husband."

"Yes," Sundara said thoughtfully. "That must be it."

"Think about it, Sundara. I've tried to keep the customs, haven't I? They say I should marry only a Khmer, but no one makes a match for me. So I find a man myself, and then they whisper it isn't right. Then I try to be a good wife and this happens." She shook her head. "I only hope we haven't started a baby. . . ."

"Yes, that would really make things difficult." Sundara looked down, noticing the cracks in Moni's cheap, poorly made shoes. *These are feet,* she thought sadly, *that have walked the length of Kampuchea.* And come to this.

"I think I must learn to steer my own boat down this river, Little Sister. I must take care of myself now. I cannot worry so much what the others say."

Maybe she was right. They walked awhile in silence. Sundara's head ached with the tension, the smoky air, the dizzying orange-and-blue geometric patterns on the carpet.

Moni spoke with a wan smile. "And what of the American boy?"

Sundara sighed. "Even when I keep my promise to stay away, my spirit is with him." She knew Soka still thought it was wrong to care for Jonathan. But now, in the new land, everyone had to make changes. Some changed more quickly than others, but in the end all had to give way to the flow. No one could keep the river from the sea.

Back at the gate, Moni went to talk to another woman and Sundara stood with Soka. They'd all run out of small talk. People were jumpy.

"Is that it?" the Khmer children would cry, running to

the windows as each plane landed. Once or twice the adults even moved toward the red double doors. Surely this was it. They gripped each other, watching. No? This was a plane from Denver? They fell back, sighing.

"I cannot endure much more of this," Soka said after the second false rush.

Grandmother, too, looked strained to the breaking point, unsteady on her feet but refusing to sit down.

Sundara touched Soka's shoulder. "She'll be here soon, Younger Aunt." She glanced around her at all the other faces, varying mixtures of anticipation and grief. The Khmers had filled an entire section of the terminal, and the white people nearby were watching them with frank curiosity.

"I wish your mother could be on the plane too," Soka said, overcome, beginning to weep with the stress of waiting. "She was my favorite sister. I don't know if she ever knew that."

Sundara thought of Mayoury. She sniffed. The little monkey . . . She could still see her with a red hibiscus blossom behind her ear, dark eyes dancing with secret mischief. Had she ever told her sister how special she was? Oh, *why* did people have to be separated before they understood how much they meant to each other? She glanced at Soka, who suddenly seemed small and vulnerable and not a person to fear at all. Would Sundara and her aunt find they cared for each other if *they* were separated?

She watched the children at the window. In their innocence this was still a party, but the adults could not help thinking of all those who would never step off a plane in the new land. Now it could never, ever be Chamroeun.

A strange thing, losing someone after such a long time of not knowing. Like the red cord binding the wrists of a wedding couple, the hope of finding him again had been one of the cords binding her to the old life in Kampuchea.

"Someday," Soka said now, "when I save up the money, I want to get a bonze to perform a ceremony for all our relatives who died. Someday when we find out for sure . . ." She shuddered. "But why am I feeling this way? This is a day to be happy. Yet somehow . . ." Suddenly she turned with a stricken look. "Sundara, what did you do with her? The baby, I mean."

Shocked, Sundara closed her eyes.

"I never wanted to ask before, but now I must know."

Sundara took a breath. "Younger Aunt, it's hard even to say it." She whispered to soften the words. "They made me throw her into the water."

"Oiee," Soka whimpered. "As I suspected, but . . . oh, my baby. No ceremony. It's just not right . . . Her little spirit wandering all this time . . ."

No ceremony. Just a small bundle splashing into the waves, just the screech of flocking gulls.

"Younger Aunt? I did pray for her."

Soka didn't answer for a moment. "I'm glad," she said finally, choking on tears. "That's better than nothing." She sniffed and looked at Sundara. "You know, you really are a good girl."

Soka's face went blurry before Sundara's eyes.

"This is the one!" Ravy yelled. "Western Airlines!"

Suddenly the group surged toward the gate, Sundara shuffling blindly with them. *Soka had called her a good girl.* Hastily she rubbed her palms up her cheeks. Tears were not the way to welcome Valinn.

The Khmers formed a human chute through which all the new arrivals would pass. The children pressed to the very door, kneeling on the blue carpet, peeking around the doorjamb. Naro motioned the group closer in one spot, back in another, nervously in charge. As the first passengers stepped out to the sea of brown faces, the Khmers leaned forward.

Two huge men in cowboy hats swaggered through. "Waiting for somebody," one drawled. "Sure as hell ain't us!" They laughed; someone whooped them a greeting.

Behind her, Sundara heard a white woman. "These orientals must be meeting a big group," she whispered.

No, Sundara thought, just one. Forty Khmers had gathered for the arrival of this one survivor. She wept openly now. No one cared, all were lost in their own emotions. If only her parents, Samet, little Mayoury . . . Through tears she read the same longing on every other face. They could have filled the entire plane with the loved ones they'd left behind.

More people came down the hall, the Khmers parting distractedly to let them pass. Somebody's grandmother, a weary couple with a whining child, a soldier with a star pinned to his uniform . . .

What if there had been a mistake? What if Valinn had missed the plane?

Then Naro whirled and started the applause. Standing on tiptoes, Sundara saw a flash of black hair and someone falling into Soka's arms. Sundara was pushed forward into the solid crush of people completely blocking the door.

"I was so scared," Valinn kept gasping in Khmer. "So scared no one would be here to meet me!" She was laughing, crying, frantically bowing to everyone, joined palms to her forehead. Sundara embraced her in turn, surprised to find her cheek pressed against the rough new denim of an American-style jacket. Where in her journey had she picked that up?

"Oh Soka," Valinn cried, "I never thought I'd see you again in this life." She embraced Soka once more and for several minutes simply cried.

"You're safe, you're safe now," Soka kept saying.

Finally, when the sobbing subsided, Valinn blinked away the tears and looked around at the children. "Which is little Sundara? I don't know her anymore."

Sundara smiled as Soka, grinning and sobbing at the same time, pulled her forward.

"But you're all grown up! And such a beauty! Oiee! I hugged you not even realizing who you were! What four or five years can do. . . ." She shook her head. "Oh, but never mind all that." She placed her palms together in front of her, eyes shining.

"Little Niece," she said, "I bring news for you."

CHAPTER 21

Sundara hurried past the city's brightly lit Christmas tree toward the riverfront plaza, hands stuffed in the pockets of her plum-colored jacket, her breath making puffs in the misty air. When she saw Jonathan waiting for her at the fountain, she broke into a run, hood falling back, hair spilling out and flying behind her as she darted between the shoppers crisscrossing the brick-paved avenue.

Jonathan looked up and spotted her. He stared as she swiftly covered the distance between them.

"Sundara," he said as she ran up and lurched to a stop, grabbing his hands. "What's happened?"

"My sister!" She was breathless, almost bouncing. "My little sister, Mayoury. She safe in a Thailand camp!"

"She's alive? That's incredible!"

"It's a miracle."

Heads turned and they dropped hands self-consciously, grinning.

"Come on," he said, and they hurried to the end of the mall, passing the fountain, skipping down the steps to the wooden view deck jutting out over the river. "When did you find out? And how? Tell me the whole thing."

"Well, yesterday we pick up my other aunt at the Portland airport. Right before she leave the Thailand camp she find Mayoury, but she cannot bring because Mayoury does not have paper yet. But some missionary promise to take care. And look." She pulled a snapshot from her jacket pocket. "See? They take a picture to prove for me she there. You know, one of those camera where the picture pop right out, you don't wait?" The print showed a child of ten or so, in a T-shirt and tattered sarong. "Look at her poor little arm and leg. She is all bone." Sundara studied the picture again. "We see so many picture of children, nothing but skin, almost stop thinking about it. But this my *sister.*"

"She's there all alone?" he asked. "What about your parents?"

Sundara hesitated. "I don't know. Maybe we find them, maybe we don't. . . ." One sad moment, then the joy flooded over her again. "But right now I just want to have this good news. Mayoury alive! A hundred way to die but she alive! Can you *believe*? Somebody put her on the back of a bicycle and ride her across Cambodia. Somebody not even family. Mayoury say a man just see her, lost and little, and he want to help." Her eyes filled.

December's early dusk was falling. With hunched shoulders and hands thrust into pockets, they watched the twinkly lights sparkling in the bare branches of the plaza's trees, thinking of a man who would help a little girl like that. No promise of repayment, no guarantee his effort would do any good. Just to help for the sake of doing the right thing.

"Already I start writing letter," Sundara went on. "I have to bring her out of there. And until I can do that, I want to send money for clothes and food through the Red Cross. Soka know how. I've got to get a job at Burger King or McDonald or something. I must prepare for her. She depending on me."

"My dad," Jonathan said. "Let's write him. Maybe he can find her."

"Ah, that would be good!"

"We got the first letter from him just today. He says your tapes are really helping."

"Oh, I'm glad. What does he say? Is it as terrible as it look on the TV?"

"It's bad, but the death rate's gone down. Says it feels good just practicing basic medicine for a change without all the tests, being able to save people."

She nodded. "You know, I think about your father and what he do. Leave your nice house where he safe, fly off. Those sick, hungry people pray to God for help, but help doesn't come from the sky, it come from the people who say, 'I think God want me to help.' People like your father and the man who help Mayoury, they kind of the answer to the prayer."

"Hmm. Maybe so." After a moment he cleared his throat, glanced at his watch. "Well . . . you better head home before somebody gets suspicious, huh? Wouldn't want you getting in trouble." He turned around and grabbed the damp wooden railing, bracing his foot against the lower bar. "I . . . it's nice of you to let me know about this."

"*Jonatan!*" She was looking at the back of his denim jacket. He didn't understand. "Don't you know you the first person I want to tell? Why you think I call you, ask you to meet me here? Why you think I run down like a crazy girl?" Still he didn't look at her. "You the one cry at my sad story, you the one gonna be happy when the good news come! You understand?"

He nodded, but when he turned back to her, his smile was still sad. "I really am happy for you, Sundara."

"Then why you look your face down like that?"

"Can't help it. It's so good to be with you again, but in a way it makes it worse, knowing things have to go back to the way they were. I just wish it wasn't so hopeless. For us, I mean."

She smiled, tilting her face. "Hopeless? You talk hopeless to me? Jonatan, you cannot talk hopeless to someone who just get a miracle. No such thing! That why I want to come share my feeling with you. It make me think, you know, *anything* can happen."

Faint hope lit his face, then faded. "Does your aunt know you're here?"

Sundara took a deep breath. "Yes. She know."

He straightened up. "And it's okay?"

Sundara watched the river churn. "She cannot stop me. I'm here." She turned to him. "Jonatan, I *have* to come, because I learn something now. Not from my family, not from the American. Just by living." She stared at the roiling brown water below them, trying to gather the courage to speak plainly.

"I learn," she whispered, "that if you love somebody . . ." Slowly she lifted her face and looked straight into his eyes, the American way. "If you love somebody, you just better let them know while you still can."

"Sundara." He took her hand, and this time she did not pull away but entwined her fingers with his.

"Five year ago," she said shyly, "I never dream that someday I stand on the bank of a river so far from the Mekong, holding the hand of an American boy. So who can ever tell about the future?"

The future was a long time, she thought, all the way down the river.

Sometimes it would be a river of deep whirlpools and treacherous shallows; she'd come too far not to know that.

But now she saw that it could also be like this, a river stretching before them clear to the horizon, broad and inviting, shimmering with hope.

ABOUT THE AUTHOR

Linda Crew and her husband, Herb, run Wake Robin Farm in Corvallis, Oregon, where they live with their three young children, Miles and twins Mary and William. Her friendships with the Cambodian refugees who work on the farm inspired her to write *Children of the River,* which won an Honorable Mention in the Fifth Annual Delacorte Press Outstanding First Young Adult Novel Contest.

She graduated from the University of Oregon and has published stories and articles in various magazines. This is her first novel.

WITHDRAWN

DATE DUE

MAY 9	1989	DEC 1	1993
MAY 16	1989	MAY 2 0	1994
		OCT 1 3	1994
MAY 3 0	1989	JAN 3 1 1995	
NOV 1 3			